Faith felt tears fill her eyes. "I don't know what to say. I—"

"Shh," he whispered, his finger against her lips again. "You don't have to say a word. Now get some sleep. You've got an incredibly busy day tomorrow."

He turned and went to the couch and began spreading out the sheets and plumping the pillow.

Faith went into her bedroom and closed the door. She'd gotten a glimpse inside the envelope when Matt had held it out. What she'd seen had turned her legs to jelly. She'd seen more hundred-dollar bills than she'd ever seen in one place in her life.

She looked at the door, feeling Matt's overwhelming presence in the next room. First he appointed himself her protector, then her personal warrior. And now this man who was by all accounts nothing more than an itinerant worker was bailing her out of debt.

As tears streamed down her face, her mind was filled with one question.

Who was Matt Soarez?

MALLORY KANE

BABY BOOTCAMP

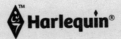

™ Harlequin®

TORONTO NEW YORK LONDON
AMSTERDAM PARIS SYDNEY HAMBURG
STOCKHOLM ATHENS TOKYO MILAN MADRID
PRAGUE WARSAW BUDAPEST AUCKLAND

To Lorraine and Debbie.
Thanks for being my true friends.

Special thanks and acknowledgment to Mallory Kane
for her contribution to the Daddy Corps series.

ISBN-13: 978-0-373-69542-3

BABY BOOTCAMP

Copyright © 2011 by Harlequin Books S.A.

Recycling programs
for this product may
not exist in your area.

ABOUT THE AUTHOR

Mallory has two very good reasons for loving reading and writing. Her mother was a librarian, who taught her to love and respect books as a precious resource. Her father could hold listeners spellbound for hours with his stories. He was always her biggest fan.

Mallory loves romantic suspense with dangerous heroes and dauntless heroines, and enjoys tossing in a bit of her medical knowledge for an extra dose of intrigue. Mallory lives in Tennessee with her computer-genius husband and three exceptionally intelligent cats.

She enjoys hearing from readers. You can write her at mallory@mallorykane.com or via Harlequin Books.

Books by Mallory Kane

CAST OF CHARACTERS

Matteo Soarez—Matt grew up hard and fast, and learned early that nothing is free.

Faith Scott—Eight months pregnant and alone, Faith has sworn she will never fall for another charming, handsome drifter.

Bart Bellows—The billionaire ex-CIA agent started Corps Security and Investigations to help young combat veterans start new lives.

Henry Kemp—This old-time cowboy has hated Texas Governor Lila Lockhart and her family ever since they struck oil on land he sold them.

Stan Lorry and Fred March—These two curmudgeons, fixtures at the Talk of the Town Café, make no bones about their dislike of Governor Lockhart, but they're all talk and mostly harmless. Or are they?

Rory Stockett—The father of Faith's baby promised her happily-ever-after, but his word was no better than the fake diamond he gave her.

Chapter One

Matt Soarez watched Faith Scott float across the chipped vinyl floor of the diner, a tray of dirty dishes in her hands and a smile on her face. She expertly maneuvered her pregnant belly between the tables and chairs, noting which coffee mugs needed refilling.

As she elbowed open the swinging door to the kitchen, she glanced briefly at Matt. The words of a Neil Young song about an unknown legend played in his head. He understood how Neil felt. Matt would gladly sit on this bar stool and order forty cups of coffee a day if that meant Faith's crystal-blue eyes would meet his forty times.

But that wasn't why he was here. Bart Bellows had given him a job in Freedom, Texas, gathering intel about the locals. According to Bellows, the Talk of the Town Café was the best place in town to hear all the local gossip.

The breakfast crowd was by far the most vocal, sharing opinions about last night's news, commenting on newspaper headlines and gossiping. Mornings were a gold mine in terms of gauging the political climate in Freedom.

Dinner conversations were very different—not nearly

as much political conversation. Early diners were there because they didn't want to cook. Matt quickly discovered that their conversations generally centered around their jobs, their families and their favorite TV shows, so after the first couple of days, he'd started coming in late, after eight o'clock, and sitting at the counter.

He was becoming an expert on people who ate in restaurants. He'd identified three types of late diners: disgruntled coworkers complaining about their awful jobs, lonely people who dreaded going home and couples in love. He learned a lot about good and bad employers in Freedom and heard intimate details he didn't need to know about some of the lovebirds.

Still, he liked this time of the day the best. He could enjoy the Talk of the Town Café's great food, and if he ordered a second piece of Faith's homemade pie, he could hang around until she closed up at nine o'clock. Sometimes, if she wasn't too busy, she talked to him.

A shout of laughter pulled his attention back to the breakfast crowd. He surveyed the room through the mirror tiles on the wall behind the counter.

Sheriff Bernard Hale was sitting in his usual spot by the window looking out onto the main street as he shoveled down his bacon and eggs. His breakfast partner, Mayor Arkwright, hadn't shown up yet. Matt glanced at his watch. Seven-thirty. Sheriff Hale was up early today.

More laughter erupted from the table directly behind Matt where two more regulars, Stan Lorry and Fred March, sat.

"Then Davidson said, 'The governor better be careful going out in the wind. If her skirt catches a breeze, her constituents might be surprised to learn—'" Lorry collapsed in laughter, unable to finish his sentence.

Fred March slapped his knee. "I don't know how he gets away with what he says on the air. I guess 'cause it's late night talk radio." He looked over at Sheriff Hale. "Hey, Sheriff? Can you arrest Allan Davidson for being too funny?"

Matt's jaw tensed. For the past week, the only variation in March and Lorry's conversations was the shock jock radio host's latest slam against Texas Governor Lila Lockhart.

"Even if I could," Hale muttered around a mouthful of eggs, "that two-bit clown would have nothing to worry about."

Stan Lorry's mouth was still stretched in a grin, but through the mirror Matt saw the harsh look he aimed at the sheriff.

"That's where you're wrong, Bernie. A lot of people think Davidson knows what he's talking about. Our dear homegrown governor's turning against the people who helped her get where she is. Davidson thinks she's wanting to run for president. He says that'll be dangerous."

Matt bit his tongue to keep from saying something. He'd been in Freedom for a week and was accepted in the way a stray dog is tolerated as long as he stays out of the way and doesn't pick a fight with the other dogs.

To these folks, he was just another itinerant construction worker, in town temporarily to work on a project at Bart Bellows's estate.

Matt couldn't risk blowing his cover.

He glanced casually at Sheriff Hale. The sheriff's eyes met his, and his head moved in an almost imperceptible shake as he lifted his mug to his lips. Matt got the message.

Let it go. Just do the job Bellows sent you here for. I'll handle these guys.

The front door opened with a jingle of the bells hung over it, and a man Matt hadn't seen before stepped in. He looked like someone's paint-by-number idea of an old cowboy, except that his jeans were new and his shirt was pressed.

"Sheriff," he said, nodding at Hale.

"Henry," the sheriff responded without looking up.

"Henry!" Stan Lorry called out. "Where you been?"

"I was down on my back for a few days, Stan. You writing a book?" Henry groused.

"Might some day," Stan shot back. "You been listening to Allan Davidson this morning?"

"I ain't got time for his nonsense," Henry said. He eyed Matt up and down, then walked up to the counter and took the stool beside him.

"Henry Kemp." He stuck his hand out.

Matt took it. "Matt Soarez," he responded.

"Soarez?" Henry let go in midhandshake. "What kind—"

"Morning, Henry," Faith said from the other side of the counter as she set a coffee mug firmly down in front of him. "Coffee?"

"Sure, honey. And my usual breakfast." Henry Kemp watched Faith fill up the mug, then turned his attention back to Matt.

"You're new around here." It sounded like an accusation.

"Yes, sir. I'm working a construction job."

"Yeah? How long you been here? Can't be more than a week, because I was in here last Tuesday."

"No, sir. Matter of fact, I got here last Tuesday night."

"Humph. Where'd you say you were working?"

"Outside of town—"

"You're working at Twin Harts, aren't you?"

At that instant, Faith set a plate of eggs, bacon and toast down in front of Kemp. He barely glanced at it.

"Do you have any idea whose place that is?" he said, his voice rising in pitch.

"Here we go," Fred March muttered.

"Actually, Mr. Kemp," Matt said, "I'm not—"

"It's our esteemed governor's family. Yep. And they're all a bunch of thieves and lowdown cowards, including her. What're you building for them? Another swimming pool? A bigger garage? More stables?" Kemp stood up and jabbed his forefinger into Matt's arm.

Matt stayed still, consciously relaxing his jaw. His job was to gather information, not cause problems. If he could control his temper through Henry Kemp's tirade, maybe he could find out exactly what the man had against the governor, because he definitely had a problem with her. So Matt wrapped his hands around his mug and didn't respond.

"I know it don't mean anything to you. You probably don't give a damn whose pockets your pay comes out of. But everything those yellowbellies own they took from me."

Kemp doubled his fist and jabbed his thumb at his own chest. "From *me!* Stole it just as sure as I'm standing here." Henry squinted at Matt, who met his gaze without speaking.

"Ah, what the hell, nobody listened to me back then, and nobody's listening to me now." He picked up his plate and his coffee and headed toward an empty table. Then he turned back.

"You, Soarez, you better watch your back. One of these days the Lockharts are going to get what's coming to them, and you don't want to be standing too close when that happens."

Sheriff Hale stood and picked up his mug. "Henry," he said with a warning note in his voice.

Kemp glowered at the sheriff.

"Isn't the twins' birthday in a few days?" Hale walked over to the table Kemp had chosen and took a seat.

Watching through the mirror, Matt had a profile view of Henry Kemp. At the sheriff's words, Henry's scowling face melted into a smile.

"Saturday," he said. "I'm bringing them here for their favorite treat—banana splits."

"How old are they going to be?"

"Four. They're like little twin dolls. Can you believe it? I remember when Lindsay was a baby herself." He looked up at Hale. "That was about the time the Lockharts beat me out of that land. Hell, sometimes it seems like yesterday." Kemp shook his head and dug into his eggs.

Matt relaxed, and he saw the sheriff's stiff back bend a little. Hale had defused a confrontation and put Kemp at ease. Seeing the aplomb with which Hale handled him, Matt figured keeping Henry Kemp from blowing his top was close to a full-time job.

"More coffee?"

Faith's melodic voice washed over Matt like a cool shower on a hot day. She was standing beside his bar stool, coffeepot in hand. He couldn't help but smile. Just looking at her soothed his eyes, and the faint scent of strawberries that surrounded her eased the tension in his jaw.

But this morning her tone was as cool as her voice—a big change from the night before, when she'd sat with him while she closed out the cash register and talked about her grandmother.

"I'd better not," he said. "Too much coffee makes for a hard day when you're working construction." He picked up the water glass and drained it, then laid several bills on the counter.

"I'm sorry about the commotion," she said. "Mr. Kemp can't let go of the past."

Matt nodded. "I got that. He resents the Lockharts for their wealth and success." Then he gave her a little salute with his coffee mug. "I'll see you this evening."

Faith's brows wrinkled slightly as she nodded, and her hand drifted across her rounded tummy in an absent, protective gesture. As he stood, she reached for his empty mug and knocked the bills to the floor.

"I'll get them," Matt said.

Faith was already crouching down. She retrieved the money and started to rise, then stopped with a little grunt of frustration.

"Here," Matt said, offering his hand. By then Lorry and March were out of their seats and Sheriff Hale was rising.

"I'm all right," Faith said evenly but accepted Matt's hand and let him pull her upright. For a beat, she stood there gripping his hand, her gaze locked on to his. Then she pulled away.

Her face turned pink as she glanced around the room

with a sheepish grin. "No more deep knee bends for me until Li'l Bit here decides to make an appearance."

Everyone laughed and went back to their breakfasts.

"Sorry," Matt said, his gaze following a strand of blond hair that escaped the braid that had slipped over her shoulder. "I didn't mean—"

"It was my fault." Faith stuck the bills into her pocket and headed around behind the counter. Her face was still bright pink.

Matt left the Talk of the Town Café and seated his Texas Rangers baseball cap on his head. After their long conversation the night before, it surprised him that Faith was so cool this morning. Did she regret telling him so much about herself? It wasn't a lot—just that her grandmother had raised her and when she'd died two years ago she'd left Faith the café with its upstairs apartment.

Maybe she was upset that he hadn't shared much about his own past. He tried to avoid talking about himself. If Faith innocently passed along any tidbits he told her, someone with money or connections might be able to trace him. If he were to be effective in uncovering the threat to Governor Lockhart, his background had to remain a mystery.

As he pressed the remote to unlock his pickup, his cell phone rang. He frowned and glanced around. Nobody nearby. He answered as he climbed into the cab and started the engine. "Soarez," he said softly.

"Soarez, it's Bellows."

Matt's shoulders straightened and his chin lifted. "Yes, sir," he responded crisply. The respect and deference due to a senior officer was ingrained in him from six years in the army.

A movement in the rearview mirror caught his eye. The front door of the café opened, and Stan Lorry stepped out, slapping his worn cowboy hat against his skinny thigh. He squinted in the direction of Matt's truck. Immediately Matt set the phone to Speaker and laid it on the console between the front seats. In his role as a construction worker, he had very little use for a cell phone.

Matt had carefully built his cover personality as a quiet man just doing his job: no pretensions, no expensive gadgets like a smartphone, not overly interested in the town except its ability to provide a good meal and a place to stay.

He consciously relaxed his shoulders as he started the pickup's engine.

"Can you talk?" Bellows asked.

"Yes, sir. I've got you on Speaker, but I'm driving in my pickup alone."

"Good. We need to meet."

Matt had only been in Freedom eight days. He'd gotten to know the names of most of the regulars at Faith's café, although this morning's encounter with Henry Kemp reminded him that he hadn't met everyone.

"Is there a problem, sir?" Matt asked. The other man's slight hesitation put him on full alert. "Sir?"

"I'll send my assistant out to get you some time this morning. You can grumble about being interrupted and afterward complain that I want an impossible change of some sort."

"Yes, sir." Matt hung up, wondering what was so important that Bellows couldn't tell him on the phone.

He drove to the renovated old stable just outside of town where he'd rented a furnished apartment. He retrieved his tools and headed for Bellows's estate.

Whatever Bellows had to tell him, it had to be something to do with the death threats Governor Lockhart and her family had been getting since rumors had surfaced that she might be considering a run for the White House.

MATT SPENT A LONG, HOT morning working on widening the turnaround in front of the Bellows' mansion. It was nearly noon, and sweat soaked the neck and back of his T-shirt and had long since seeped through the bandanna he used as a headband. When he stopped to wipe sweat from his eyes, someone tapped him on the shoulder.

Matt turned.

The man, dressed in a summer-weight suit, jerked a thumb back toward the house. "Need to see you," he growled.

A couple of workers stopped to look curiously toward Matt.

Matt finished wiping his face, shrugged and set his spade down. "I'll just wash up…" he started, but the large man shook his head.

"Now."

With a glance and a shrug at his fellow workers that said, *Bosses, what are you going to do,* Matt followed the man around the house to an entrance he hadn't noticed. It was nestled into the side of the house and looked as much like a window as a door.

The large man opened the door and stood back to let Matt enter, then closed it behind him. After being in the bright sun outside, the room was pitch-black. It took his eyes a few seconds to adapt to the darkness. Once they did, he saw a desk lamp's glow reflecting off the curved metal wheels of a wheelchair. He stepped closer.

Bellows had been a big man—an imposing man—at one time. Even now his shock of white hair, brushed back from a receding hairline, lent him an air of wisdom and dignity. The sense was aided by his excellent posture, gray beard and sharp blue eyes. He was dressed in a suit and string tie and tooled leather cowboy boots. A white Stetson sat on his lap.

"Sir," Matt said. "I apologize for—" he held his palms out, embarrassed by his sweat-stained shirt and pants and his dusty work boots.

"Bah. Appearances." Bellows waved an elegant, long-fingered hand. "Sit down, son. Sit."

Matt perched carefully on the edge of a straight-backed chair and prepared to listen.

"How's it going? Are the people in Freedom accepting you?"

"A lot of them are still skittish since the two deaths at the Fourth of July parade. In fact, quite a few blame Governor Lockhart, because her daughter was involved. But I've managed to stay under the radar. I'm just an itinerant worker who eats every meal at the Talk of the Town Café."

"Speaking of Governor Lockhart, that's why I needed to see you. We've got a problem."

"Yes, sir?"

"She's decided she wants to hold a town hall meeting in Freedom."

Matt frowned. "A town hall meeting? When?"

"On Saturday, three days from now."

"Three days? But I thought we had plenty of time

before she made her final decision to run for president."

Bellows sighed. "She declares that she's not planning to announce anything. She just wants to—as she puts it—feel out the town. Freedom is where her family has lived for generations. And Eliza Scott's café is where she announced that she was running for governor years ago. She has a special fondness in her heart for Freedom."

Matt heard the resigned note in Bellows's voice. He leaned forward and propped his elbows on his knees. He studied the older man. "You think she's going to use the meeting to make her candidacy official."

"It's hard to predict what Lila's going to do. She's as stubborn as a mule on a hot August day. If I thought announcing her bid for president was all this is about, I'd be happy. I'm worried her intent is to thumb her nose at whoever is sending these threatening messages to her. They're continuing to escalate."

"Well, at least the danger to her daughter wasn't connected," Matt said. "Bailey's safe now."

"Yes, for now. But it cost two people their lives and upset the people of Freedom." Bellows brushed an imaginary speck of dust off the brim of the hat in his lap. "I'm afraid the bloodshed may not be over. The tone of these threats has gone from warning to deadly. That's why I needed to talk to you in person. Stay around town between now and Saturday. Tell folks the construction project is on hold. You can work with the governor's crew, preparing the venue. I want you right there before, during and after the meeting. You'll spot potential threats and notify Sheriff Hale, who'll have his deputies watching the crowd, along with Lila's bodyguards and a couple of officers from the Amarillo P.D."

Matt ran his fingers through his close-cropped hair. "How many bodyguards will the governor have?"

"Not sure. But you'll be in direct contact with Hale. If anybody does anything to disrupt the meeting, your top priority is identifying the culprit. Lila's bodyguards and the police will take care of her."

"When will the governor get there, and when will she leave?"

"She hasn't said. I'm hoping she'll fly back to Austin Saturday night, but I have a feeling she's going to stay at Twin Harts for a few days." Bart Bellows shook his head. "Any other questions?"

"The meeting will be held at the old town hall?"

"Nope. Like I said, Lila made her announcement of running for governor at the Talk of the Town Café, and that's where she wants to hold this meeting."

"But—" Matt thought about Faith, pregnant and tired and already working from six o'clock in the morning until after nine at night "—the café can't hold more than sixty people."

"Hey, don't tell me. You're preaching to the choir here. Lila keeps reminding me that last time there couldn't have been more than seventy to a hundred people there and that Eliza opened the double doors leading to the street so people could stand out there and hear the speech."

Matt shook his head. "But the governor is not an unknown wannabe trying her hand at politics this time. Once the word gets out about this Freedom is going to be overrun with pro-Lockhart and anti-Lockhart factions, curiosity seekers and media."

"Nothing's going to change Lila's mind. I need you to treat this as an encounter in hostile territory. Your mission is to identify the threat and neutralize it. Use the skills and tactics that made you a decorated surveillance expert in the army."

At Bellows's words, Matt's brain was suddenly awash with memories of hot, dusty streets, a few burka-clad women scattering to get out of the way of the jeeps and ragged children. The kids shouted and waved at the soldiers, wanting coins or food. Matt was riding in the second vehicle, armed and ready for anything, although scouting reports had described the village as nearly abandoned.

He glanced at the kids one more time, then turned his attention to the high windows and mud roofs. Just because the reports didn't find any danger didn't mean there wasn't any. But the roofs were clear—no glint of sun on a rifle barrel, no odd movements along the roof lines.

Out of the corner of his eye, he saw a tiny boy, no more than four or five, run up close to the lead vehicle. His mother was right behind him. She grabbed his arm and sprinted away, half dragging the child out of the way of the vehicles.

But something wasn't right. She'd paused a fraction of a second with her back to the other vehicles.

Matt's gaze snapped to the side of the jeep where she'd stood.

There it was.

"Bomb!" he'd shouted, but it was too late. The deafening blast had drowned out his voice. His first thought was of his best friend Rusty in the lead jeep. His second was of all the women and children.

"Soarez?"

Matt blinked. "Yes, sir."

"Something wrong? A problem with your assignment?"

"No, sir. I've got it."

"How's your knee?"

"No problem, sir," Matt said. "I can run just fine."

"I know. That's what your discharge orders say. My question is will it hold up in hand-to-hand combat? Or quick changes in pace or direction?"

Matt resisted the urge to reach down and rub his knee. "A hundred percent, sir."

Bellows studied Matt for a long moment, then jabbed the air near his arm with a pointed finger. "You and I both know that knee is not a hundred percent. If it was, you'd still be in the army. People who lie to me are useless to me." Bellows put his hands on the wheels of his chair and rolled it backward a few inches. "Now, do you want to rethink that answer, or do you want to get your stuff and head back to L.A.? What'll it be, Sergeant Soarez?"

Chapter Two

Matt's back stiffened, and he cringed at the word *lie*. He felt heat rise from his neck to his face.

"I apologize, sir," he answered Bellows. "My knee has around sixty percent mobility. It's nearly a hundred percent on straight line running, but I'd probably throw it out playing guard on a basketball court where I'd have to be sidestepping a great deal."

"That's better," Bellows said. "What's your plan for handling surveillance at the town hall meeting?"

"Well, sir," Matt said, picturing the diner's layout in his mind, "I'd like to have policemen at the front doors and covering the door from the kitchen to the alley. I'd barricade the basement storage room and the stairs leading up to Faith's apartment. The whole front of the café is glass, and we don't have enough manpower to block it all, so I'd just let the locals and possibly the media stand in that area. Whoever is after Governor Lockhart probably isn't interested in hurting innocent people. He'll have a plan that focuses on his specific target—the governor. He won't have the time or the manpower to do anything but hit and run."

Bellows's sharp eyes met Matt's. "Makes sense. And where will you be?"

"I'll be on stage with the governor. I need to face the crowd—see their faces, their eyes."

"Not a bad plan, off the top of your head."

"Thank you, sir." Matt paused. "We'll need communications units. Tasers would be nice, so we can target any disruptors without hurting civilians."

"I can arrange that. Now tell me what you've learned about the good people of Freedom."

Matt thought back over the eight days he'd been in town. "Sheriff Hale is a good man. I'd feel comfortable depending on him to cover my back. His deputy, Appleton, is a single father with a six-year-old. I'm not sure how much risk he'd take. The sheriff's other deputies are pretty much what you'd expect—generally competent but nothing extraordinary."

Bellows sat back in his chair and tented his fingers, listening.

"The mayor's no fan of the governor," Matt went on, "but he's got more ambition than conviction, so I'm sure he's not above riding her coattails."

Bellows nodded, showing tacit agreement with Matt's assessments.

"The attitudes about the governor's daughter, Bailey, are mixed. Most people like her a lot and are happy that she's okay and is getting married. Apparently there are others who think she shouldn't have stayed here knowing she could be putting townspeople in danger."

"Who said that?"

"Well, according to Stan Lorry and Fred March, who hang out at the café all morning, a talk radio host named Allan Davidson devoted one whole show to the subject of Bailey Lockhart and the Fourth of July shootings. He got dozens of phone calls from people in Freedom.

Lorry and March think Davidson is the greatest thing since sliced bread."

"I'll get a transcript of that show and see who called in. Anyone else?"

"I met Henry Kemp for the first time this morning. He's a wild card. He has a burr under his saddle about the Lockharts." Matt paused.

Bellows raised a shaggy eyebrow.

"He made a threat against them."

"A threat? What kind of threat?"

"This morning was the first time I've ever met him, so it could be that he's just a blowhard. But his exact words to me were 'One of these days the Lockharts are going to get what's coming to them, and you don't want to be too close when that happens.'"

"Yeah, that sounds like Henry. He's been telling his tale of woe about the Lockharts stealing his oil rights for two decades. Nothing's ever his fault. He can always find someone else to blame. He's got no legal claim to the oil rights on the land he sold to the Lockharts. It was just his bad luck that the oil was discovered by them and not him. What do you think about him?"

Matt thought back to Kemp's florid, angry face and the look in his eyes. "He's obsessed with them. He's volatile. I think he could resort to violence."

"He's got a beautiful granddaughter and twin great-granddaughters that he worships. Why would he risk their safety and happiness by going after the Lockharts?"

Matt frowned. Was Bellows testing him? "Just my opinion, sir," he said stiffly.

Bellows's eyes sparked. "You're going to have to do better than that, Sergeant Soarez. I know we don't know each other well, but when I ask a question I expect a straight answer. You think I'm baiting you, that I know the answer I want from you and I'm testing you."

The old man cleared his throat. "Well, this is no test. If I'd wanted people who agreed with me, I'd have hired lawyers. You're here because you're a decorated combat veteran, a hero. You have a set of skills I need, and your opinion matters to me. I need to know I can count on you to give me a straight answer, no matter what that answer is."

"Sir, I—"

"Listen son. I get that you don't trust me, and I get why," Bellows went on. "You came up like I did—hard, alone. You figured out how to protect yourself. And you learned early that nothing is free and no one can be trusted."

At Bellows's statement that he understood Matt's childhood, Matt tried to quell an urge to laugh. He caught himself but not in time.

"You don't think I get it? Hell, son, I don't give a damn whether you think I had a hard life or not. What I *do* give a damn about is whether I can trust you. From your background and your military service, I already know that you're loyal and trustworthy. You were top of your field in surveillance. But you aren't being straight-forward with me."

Matt thought back. "About my knee, sir?"

"Tell you what, son, you think about it while you answer this. Why are you here? Why did you accept this job? Of the men I invited to work for me, you were the most reluctant, even though I threw in full scholarships for your twin sisters to the colleges of their choice."

Matt wondered what would happen if he told Bellows

the truth. He was bound by a contract. Bellows had made it a deal breaker. So he was on board for at least three months, during which time Bellows would evaluate him for the permanent Core Security and Investigations, or CSAI, team. Matt had no idea what kind of deal the other agents had been given, but Bellows was asking for straight answers from him. He took a deep breath.

"I don't like being in debt," he said. "I went into the army because it was good money. Now I'm out and waiting to hear if I qualify for disability and if so how much. I've got a knee that's never going to work right, and I'm unemployed. As you just mentioned, I have a certain skill set that's pretty useless outside of combat.

"Then you come along and give me an offer that's too good to be true. I definitely took it because of the money. There's no way I could afford to send my sisters to college otherwise. And I'm tired of watching my mother work so hard for so little pay. I need this job. But if you try to leverage me using my mother or my sisters, Mr. Bellows, you'll be sorry. My family is off-limits." Matt stopped and waited for the explosion, but Bellows's expression never changed.

"So what are you saying? You turning down the scholarships for your sisters?" Bellows asked.

Matt swallowed. The money Bellows had dangled over him as a salary was more than Matt had dreamed of ever making. But it wasn't enough to put his seventeen-year-old twin sisters through college. They'd be the first Soarezes to graduate college, if he could scrape up the money. "The salary you offered me was beyond generous. Why throw in full scholarships?"

"Because I needed you, and I knew I could manipulate you by helping your family. You've heard the old saw about looking a gift horse in the mouth, haven't you?"

"You've heard that if it seems too good to be true, then it probably is."

Bellows wrapped his hands around the wheels of his chair and turned it away from Matt.

Matt's breath caught in his throat. Had he just talked himself out of a job?

Bellows wheeled over to the big mahogany desk and maneuvered his chair behind it. Then he reached into a drawer and pulled out a slender file.

"Over three years ago, I decided that I wanted to do something more with my life, so I created Corps Security and Investigations. I met a young war veteran who had nearly died in a roadside bombing. I asked for his help, and in return I gave him mine."

"The man we met in Dallas," Matt guessed. "The man you call Nolan Law."

Bellows nodded. "We spent months working on our mission statement, its purpose and its function. There were hundreds of details to be worked out. Once we were ready, we acquired the service records of one hundred and twenty-three veterans who had seen active combat and who lived in or close to Texas. After serious review and lots of debate, we narrowed the list to five."

Bellows tapped a finger on the slender file. "This is your service record, as well as a summary of all public records involving you and your family."

Matt wanted nothing more than to charge the wheelchair-bound man, grab his records and vamoose. But he clenched his fists and stood his ground. Obviously Bellows had a point to make.

"I can understand why you might think our offer is too good to be true. But let me assure you right now that it's not. You're going to work—harder than you've ever worked in your life—to earn the money and benefits I've offered you. You'll be required to lay your life on the line, maybe not as often or as frighteningly as when you were in combat, but Corps Security and Investigations is an elite team of men with special skills. Each of you was selected because of what you can do. You do not have a backup. That means if you've worked twenty days straight without a break and I need a surveillance expert, you'll work twenty more."

Bellows rolled out from behind the desk again and looked Matt straight in the eye. "If you remember, your contract states that your life is insured for five hundred thousand dollars. If you die while performing your duties, your beneficiaries will receive a lump sum payout, no questions asked. But that payout marks the end of the contract. Do you still think your proposed salary plus benefits is 'too good to be true'?"

Matt swallowed. Bellows seemed genuinely passionate about his company. Maybe the job was legitimate after all.

"Okay then, I need you to talk to Sheriff Hale and coordinate crowd containment and security during and after the town hall meeting."

"Yes, sir."

"Now, before you leave, please correct your second misleading statement."

Thinking back, Matt realized what Bellows was talking about. "Yes, sir. I believe Henry Kemp has compartmentalized his separate lives. On the one hand, he's a loving grandfather. On the other, he's an avenger, out to right what he feels is a grave injustice. He can't comprehend that destroying the Lockharts will destroy his own family."

Bellows's mouth twitched at the corners. "That's more like it. I'll have someone on Henry Kemp during the town hall meeting. You keep an eye out for any other suspicious characters. Remember, your number one priority is keeping Governor Lockhart alive."

FAITH SCOTT STARED AT the portable phone handset she held. A twinge on the right side of her rounded belly made her jump. She rubbed the spot. "Sorry, Li'l Bit. I'm a little frazzled. I just found out that you and I are going to be really busy for the next few days."

"Faith? Faith!" It was Glo, shouting from the storeroom downstairs.

Faith walked over to the door leading to the stairs. "What? Are you okay?"

"Was that the telephone? It better not have been Valerio. He's already late. If he doesn't walk through that door in the next thirty seconds, he's not going to be able to walk. I can't lift these cases of mayonnaise by myself, and I'm not traipsing up and down the stairs eight times when he can lift two cases at once."

Faith looked at the wooden stairs descending down into the darkness and sighed. Normally, she could easily bring two or three gallons up by herself, but not now—not with a baby on board. "I'll come halfway down, and you can hand me one jar at a time."

"Hell, no, you won't!" Gloria McDonald yelled. "You stay right there."

Faith heard Glo's tennis shoes thudding up the stairs. At the same time, the back door opened and closed and

Valerio Rodriguez pushed through the swinging door from the kitchen, snagging the apron that hung beside it.

"Ah, *mi ave blanca*. You are so beautiful today." It was his usual greeting. "I am here, ready for anything." He slipped the apron over his head and tied the strings behind his waist.

Gloria McDonald, dressed in a white uniform with a green apron and glistening red lipstick, rose from the dark staircase like a kraken from the depths of the ocean.

"There you are, Valerio. Get your lazy butt down the stairs and bring up two cases of mayonnaise. You should have brought them up yesterday. Faith ran out last night and had to go down there and get a jar."

"*Perdón*," Valerio said to Faith, then turned to Glo. "You need mayonnaise so desperately and yet you came up the stairs empty-handed?" He spread his hands. "Ah, poor Glori-ah. I know you're terribly old and decrepit, but even those flabby arms could lift one jar."

"Listen, you big windbag, I can beat you to a pulp with one hand tied behind my back. You just name the place and time. Go ahead, name it."

"Glo," Faith said as Valerio let fly a string of probably insulting Spanish. "Valerio—"

"Yeah? Well, right back at you!" Glo snapped.

"Both of you, be quiet!" Faith yelled.

Glo and Valerio turned to stare at Faith, open-mouthed. Faith gathered her long, wavy hair with both hands and lifted it off her neck. It seemed to ease the ache between her shoulder blades.

"I'm sorry," she said, letting her hair fall. "But I need to tell you something."

Glo's red cheeks cooled down, and the tendons in Valerio's neck began to recede.

"What is it, honey?" Glo asked, looking Faith up and down. "Your water didn't break, did it?"

"Here." Valerio dragged a chair over. "Sit, *nueva madre*. I'll get you a glass of water."

"No! Just stop a minute and listen." Faith felt the baby stirring restlessly. She rubbed the side of her belly. "You'll never believe who that was on the phone just now."

"Who?" Glo and Valerio said in unison.

"The governor's public relations agent. According to her, the governor wants to hold a town hall meeting here on Saturday." Saying it out loud made it sound even more impossible than it had through the phone line from Governor Lockhart's PR officer. She shook her head.

"In Freedom?" Valerio said.

Glo frowned. "Here?" she asked.

Faith lifted her hair again. She was hot and tired and trying her best to tamp down the panic that was pushing its way up her throat. "Here," she squeaked. "At the café." She took a deep breath. "I guess I could use some water."

Valerio rushed around the counter and filled a glass with ice and water and slid it toward her. She picked it up and drank gratefully. The chill liquid soothed her parched throat. "Apparently, when she first decided to run for governor, she announced it here. I don't remember that. Anyhow, she wants to hold a meeting here Saturday." Some water spilled out of the glass she held. That's how badly her hands were shaking.

"That's right," Glo said. "It must have been about ten years ago. I guess you were about fifteen and giving your grandmother a hard time. As I recall, it wasn't that big a deal. We closed for dinner that night and opened the double doors in front so everyone could hear her talk. Someone brought in a microphone and speakers."

Faith shook her head. "Well, it's going to be a big deal this time. The café only holds sixty people, and the governor's PR person said they were going to have TV and news crews here and they'd wire the place for sound, with loudspeakers outside so everyone can hear."

She picked up the water glass again, and the ice cubes tinkled noisily. "I don't know how we're going to handle it."

"What else did the person say?"

"She said they were going to take care of everything, but I'm afraid—"

"Well, then let them," Glo declared. "All you need to do is stay out of their way."

"But it's my café. I should provide water or coffee—?"

"No, you shouldn't," Glo insisted. "If the governor thinks she can waltz in here and disrupt everything without so much as a by-your-leave, then she's responsible for making things go smoothly."

"Glori-ah?" Valerio said. "What about the threats on the governor's life?"

Glo sent Valerio an impatient look. "Rumors. That's all. Everybody who ever ran for office in this state has had at least one threat against them. Hell, *everybody* in the state's probably got somebody who'd rather they weren't around."

The panic Faith had managed to quell was trying to rise again. "Threats? I know there was that man who was stalking Bailey, but—?"

Chapter Three

Despite her best intentions of grabbing just a catnap, Faith slept for a couple of hours and didn't make it downstairs until after seven. By that time, dinner was in full swing. Almost everyone was eating the special. Valerio's tequila-lime roast chicken was a café favorite.

Glo winked at Faith as she carried trays laden with plates of chicken, baskets of rolls and drinks. Faith looked at the pass through window and saw three more plates waiting to be delivered to their tables.

"Two to table seven," Glo called out, "and one to the counter."

Faith glanced at the customer sitting at the counter and saw that it was Matt Soarez. His dark eyes met her gaze and he gave a brief nod.

She didn't like the way she felt when he looked at her. Her heart fluttered like a teenaged girl's, while at the same time a frisson of fear slid through her. She recognized both sensations, but the fear quickly killed the flutter, because it made her think of Rory Stockett, her baby's father.

Deliberately ignoring Matt's nod of greeting, she grabbed the plate of chicken and set it in front of him, then topped off his iced tea. By that time, Glo was back and taking the other two plates.

"Glo, I've got those," Faith said, but Glo shook her head.

"You cut the pies. I've already got two orders for apple with caramel pecan ice cream."

The next hour was busy, but by eight-thirty, all the diners had cleared out except Matt. As soon as the dishes where piled into the dishwasher and the leftovers were thrown out, Faith sent Glo and Valerio home.

"Molly's coming in early tomorrow," she told them, "and I feel great. You two need to get some rest. Neither one of you has had a day off in over a week."

"I don't need a day off," Glo protested.

Valerio said, "I'm happy to get overtime."

Faith held up her hand. "I need both of you to be in top form when I go to the hospital. So please, don't overdo it now."

Glo and Valerio looked at each other, then back at Faith, but before they could open their mouths, she said, "End of discussion. By the way Glo, could you pick up a Help Wanted sign tomorrow? Molly's going back to school in a couple of weeks, and I need to hire someone to take her place."

"Sure thing, hon," Glo said.

When Glo and Valerio finally left, Faith locked the back door behind them and made herself a cup of hot tea. As the tea was steeping, she leaned against the stainless steel table and rubbed the right side of her belly, which still ached. Her eyes pricked with tears. This time of night, after the café was closed and everything was quiet, was the loneliest time of her day. It's when she missed Gram the most.

"Oh, Gram," she murmured. "I let you down. You were right. Men are like butterflies."

She smiled although her eyes were filled with tears as Gram's words came back to her.

Most men are like butterflies, Faith honey. They're pretty and you want to follow them, but sooner or later they'll end up leading you into... at that moment Gram would pause and then say delicately, *manure.*

Faith would always ask about her grandpa. *But Grandpa was different. Right, Gram?*

Gram would get a faraway look in her eye. *Your grandpa was one in a million, Faith. One in a million. I hope you can find one, but you may have to let a lot of butterflies go by.*

"Don't worry, Gram," Faith murmured as she stroked the side of her tummy. "No more butterflies. Once I get the loan paid off, Li'l Bit and I are going to be just fine by ourselves."

She blinked the tears away and picked up her teacup. Enough feeling sorry for herself. She still needed to lock the front door and close out the cash register.

She heard the slight squeak of the swinging door, and a low masculine voice said, "Busy night."

Faith started and almost spilled her cup. It was Matt. She'd forgotten he was still here. She didn't look at him, afraid the traces of tears were visible on her face.

"Busy is a good thing," she said. "The busier we are, the sooner I can pay off the loan."

"Loan?"

Faith bit her tongue. *Damn it.* That had slipped out because it was on her mind.

She'd been so careful not to let anyone in town know that she'd been stupid enough to believe Rory Stockett's lies. She slid past him and through the door out into the dining area.

Matt followed behind.

"I got the impression your grandmother left you this place free and clear."

Faith almost laughed. She looked at him, steeling herself against the fluttering of her heart and the sinking feeling in her stomach. "Nothing's free, Mr. Soarez."

Matt smiled, but his eyes narrowed assessingly. "I thought you were going to call me Matt."

"Matt," she said reluctantly, wishing she hadn't sat and talked with him the night before. She didn't know anything about him, but she knew all about his type. He was a butterfly if ever she'd seen one.

He was in town temporarily, working a construction job. He was handsome and charming, and when he looked at her with those dark, soulful eyes, he made her feel like the most beautiful, desirable girl in the world—just like Rory had. And just like Rory, he'd be gone within a few weeks.

But at least *this* charming drifter wouldn't stomp on her heart as he walked away because he wouldn't get near it.

"Was there something else you wanted? Because I need to close up," she said pointedly.

He shook his head. "I just wanted to be sure you're all right. Glo said you weren't feeling well."

Faith took a step backward and rubbed the side of her tummy. "I'm just tired. It's been a long day, and it's going to be a very long weekend."

He looked at his watch. "It's not very late. You want me to make you a fresh cup of tea?"

"Make me—?" At first the words didn't even make

sense. Nobody made tea for her—not since Gram died. "No. I mean—"

She looked at him. He was a lot taller than her but not as tall as Rory or as thin. Matt was lean but solid. His chest and abs were obvious beneath the white T-shirt he wore, and the muscles in his arms were sharply defined. Dark jeans hinted at powerful thighs. The impression he gave was that he'd never start a fight, but he wouldn't turn away either.

And he wouldn't lose.

"Hey," he said, amused. "I can make tea. I can even cook a few things." His brows lowered. "Speaking of cooking, when did you eat?"

Faith set her cup down. "I had a— I think it was—" She stopped. When had she eaten last?

"Okay, that settles it. I'm fixing you some dinner. Want some of the chicken special? A cheese quesadilla? Some eggs?"

"No." She shook her head. "It's late."

"No, it's not. It's a long time until breakfast."

"It may not be late for you, but I still have to close out the cash register, review the credit card receipts to be sure there are no duplications, clean off the tables and check the salt and pepper shakers and—oh," she stopped. On the far table, near the door to the basement, was a huge dishpan of dirty dishes. Glo had missed them while she was cleaning up.

"—and wash another load of dishes."

Matt swiveled on his seat, checking out the loaded pan. "I'll get that for you." He looked back at her. "Why aren't your employees here helping you with all this?"

"Because I made them go home. Glo has worked eight days straight without a day off, and Valerio will be here at 4:00 a.m. to start the chicken stock and the dough for the rolls."

Matt got up off the stool, laid a twenty on the counter and headed to the back table to get the pan full of dishes.

Faith took his twenty and put his change back on the counter, then started sorting through the credit card receipts. "Thanks for helping with the dishes. Put them on the table in the kitchen."

"I'll load them in the dishwasher and turn it on," Matt said, coming around the counter.

"There are clean dishes in the dishwasher. And the mechanism's tricky. I'll get it."

"Faith, I've worked in my share of diners and restaurants. Let me do this for you."

She sighed and gave a little shrug. "Fine. Thank you," she said grudgingly.

"And while I'm in here, I'll make you some eggs and a hot cup of tea."

As he pushed through the swinging door, she got a sharp pain in her right side. "Come on, Li'l Bit. Settle down. We'll get to sleep soon."

Pulling out the calculator from the shelf beneath the cash register, Faith began adding up the credit card receipts for the day, checking each one to be sure the math was correct and all the information was clearly readable.

The verification of the credit card receipts was a long, tedious process, but her customers depended on her to make sure there were no mistakes. A couple of times Faith's eyelids threatened to close, but the smell of scrambled eggs and toast wafting in from the kitchen made it obvious that she was hungrier than she was sleepy.

About the time she was done with the cash register receipts, and her stomach was growling in anticipation of Matt's scrambled eggs, the bells above the door jingled.

Faith looked up and gasped. Standing in the doorway was a tall, handsome man with dark wavy hair that was a fraction of an inch too long and a smile that was a fraction of an inch too wide.

For a second, Faith couldn't do anything but gape. She hadn't seen him since she'd taken out the loan for him. She'd figured she'd never seen him again, but here he was. Her stomach sank all the way to her toes.

"Rory!" she croaked through a throat that was tight with disbelief.

Rory Stockett swaggered in. "Hey, babe," he said.

Faith stared at him as he came closer. "What are you doing here?"

"Wow, you're looking good," Rory continued as if she hadn't spoken. He headed her way, then stopped short.

"Whoa!" A fleeting grimace crossed his face. "Look at you. You're about to pop, aren't you?"

Anger and resentment washed over her. "No, I am not about to pop. That's a disgusting thing to say, especially since you haven't shown your face around here in almost six months."

His cloying cologne nearly gagged her as he leaned over the counter to kiss her. She recoiled.

His eyes snapped with irritation. "Hey, Faith, what the hell? I figured you'd be glad to see me. Didn't you miss me?"

His eyes went to the open cash register drawer, then back to her. He gave her his most charming grin.

"You really do look good. I guess pregnancy agrees with you. What have we got there? A little boy? A girl?" He reached out a hand toward her tummy.

Faith stiffened and took a step backward. "*We* don't have anything, remember? You need to leave. I've got to close up and balance the register."

"Looks like you're doing a good business. I'm glad."

Faith's hand tightened on the credit card receipts she held. The dread weighing on her stomach told her Rory was here for one thing only—money. Hadn't she already shown him she was an easy touch? "Please go, Rory."

"Okay, Faith. I'll confess. I really wanted to see you. I've missed you a lot, more than you can imagine. But I—I couldn't face you after what happened." He paused, watching her face, but she didn't change expressions.

"I got crossed up on my trucking business. A guy I trusted took my money and didn't deliver on the rig he promised me. He gave me a broken down vehicle that wasn't worth a quarter of what I paid him."

Faith pressed her lips together. She wished Rory would leave before Matt came out of the kitchen. For some reason, she didn't want Matt to see Rory Stockett. He'd have him sized up within five seconds, and she wasn't sure she could take the look of disdain he'd send her way while he tried to figure out how she could be so dumb.

"Listen, babe," Rory continued, his voice changing into the wheedling tone she hated. "I've missed you so much. I want to take care of you and our baby, but I need a favor. I'm a little short, and I've got a really good deal lined up. Can you let me have a few hundred? Say five? I swear I can triple it in a couple of weeks."

"No!" Faith snapped. "Get out of here. I was fool enough to believe you once but never again. I wouldn't loan you a life preserver if you were drowning," she cried, knowing she would. No matter what a lowdown con man he was, he was also her child's father.

"Hey, come on. Five C-notes? You pull in more than that at breakfast." He reached into the register and grabbed a handful of twenties.

Faith reacted instantaneously, slamming the drawer on his hand.

"Ow!" he screeched, jerking his hand away and shaking it. His face turned red. He bared his teeth, then he grabbed her hair.

"That hurt!" He jerked her up against him, knocking her belly against the wooden counter.

"Rory, stop," she cried. "You'll hurt the baby."

His fist tightened, burning her scalp and bringing tears to her eyes. He growled.

Faith pushed against his chest with all her might, but he outweighed her by at least forty pounds.

"Rory! Stop!" she cried again, only to be rewarded by Rory bending her neck backward with the strength of his hold on her hair.

Suddenly, Rory's guttural growl changed into a gurgle. His grip on her hair loosened.

Jerking her head and feeling strands of hair pull out because they were wrapped around his fingers, Faith propelled herself backward as far as she could. She didn't know what had happened to make him let go, but she was taking advantage of it. She blinked against tears as she scooted out of grabbing distance of Rory.

Hazily, she took in the scene before her. She'd had to call Sheriff Hale to break up arguments at the café, but this was the first time she'd ever seen a real brawl.

Matt had a headlock on Rory and was pinching his left elbow with his free hand. Rory was squealing and batting ineffectually at Matt's arm with his right fist.

After a few seconds, Rory's hand went slack, and the wad of twenties drifted to the floor. Then Matt swung the taller man around and slammed him against the door facing with his forearm pressing into his Adam's apple. Rory's face was beet-red and headed toward purple.

"Matt, let him go," Faith cried. She was afraid Matt could kill Rory.

Matt put a little more weight behind his forearm. Rory struggled to breathe. "I don't know who you are, but you lay a hand on her again and you'll have to learn to live without it. Understand?" Matt let up a bit on the pressure, enough that Rory could speak.

Rory sucked in a deep rasping breath. "You son of a—"

Matt pressed again. "Faith, call Sheriff Hale. Tell him we have an attempted robbery over here."

Rory's eyes bulged, and he shook his head. Sweat was beading on his forehead and dripping down his temples.

Faith was too shaken to think. She went to the phone, but for the life of her she couldn't remember the sheriff's telephone number.

"Ack!" Rory gurgled.

"Yeah? You ready to leave and not come back?"

Rory nodded. Matt eased up on the pressure against Rory's throat. Immediately, Rory's hand went to his neck. "You son of a bitch," he muttered. "You could have killed me."

Matt nodded congenially. "That's right. But I didn't. Faith, you can tell the sheriff we don't need him now."

Faith looked at the handset she held, then hung it up.

Matt shoved Rory toward the front door. "Don't ever come back in here."

Rory turned and looked at Faith. "It didn't take you long to find another sucker, did it? Did you tell him that baby's mine?"

"She's not yours," Faith snapped. "She's *mine*."

Matt lifted his chin and took a step toward Rory.

He swallowed and opened the door. Then he turned back. "You, whoever you are, you're going to be sorry you messed with me." He looked past Matt to Faith. "And so will you, bitch!" He slammed the door.

Matt switched the sign from Open to Closed, locked the dead bolt and lowered the blinds. Then he turned around. Faith was pale as a ghost and wavering on her feet. He rushed over to her side.

"Here," he said. "Sit down for a few minutes. Did he hurt you?"

She shook her head. "Not as badly as I hurt him. I slammed the cash register drawer on his hand. I hope I broke a finger."

"Good for you. That's the baby's father?"

Faith lowered her head and nodded. "Rory Stockett. He drifted into town looking for work and started hanging around the café. He was…sweet, attentive." She clasped her fingers together tightly and stared at them.

Matt looked at the top of her blond head and the

delicate slope of her shoulders. Her description of Stockett was a perfect fit for him as well. As far as she knew, Matt was just another sweet, attentive drifter.

It explained a lot about her warm and cool running emotions.

He found it so easy to talk to her. It seemed that whenever they were together they just slipped into pleasant, comfortable conversation. But invariably, after a few minutes, Faith would start backing away—sometimes physically, always emotionally. Now he understood why. She saw him as another man like her ex. As much as he longed to tell her—to show her—that he was no drifter, that unlike Stockett, he was trustworthy, he couldn't.

Although, even if she knew the truth, would she see him as any more honest than Stockett? He was lying to her as surely as Stockett had.

He shook his head mentally and reminded himself that it didn't matter if she trusted him. He was here to do a job, and part of that job involved keeping her safe. Bellows needed the Talk of the Town Café, and the café existed because of Faith.

Faith was still visibly shaken. The fingers of one hand were covering her mouth, and the other hand rubbed the side of her tummy.

Matt sat down across from her. "What did he do to you?" he asked softly.

"He grabbed my hair when I slammed the drawer on his hand. That's all."

"No," Matt said, taking her hand away from her mouth and enclosing it in his. "Not tonight. What happened before?"

She looked at their clasped hands for a few seconds then raised her head and gave him a rueful smile. "Same old story," she said. "Boy meets girl. Girl gets pregnant. Boy gives girl a ring and asks for money to start a trucking business so they can have a good life. Girl's too gullible to see through him. Boy skips town with the money." She shrugged.

Matt's chest ached for her. She'd believed in Rory Stockett, and he'd taken advantage of her. "How often does he show up like this?"

"Never," she said. "I thought he was gone for good. I haven't seen him since the day I gave him the money."

"And he shows up tonight. Why now?" Right before the big town hall meeting? It could be a coincidence, but Matt had a hard time believing that. He needed to check with Bellows, see what he knew about Rory Stockett.

"What do you mean, why now?"

Matt straightened. "I've heard rumors that Governor Lockhart is planning to be in Freedom this weekend. What are Stockett's political leanings?"

Faith laughed. "He doesn't have any. Nor does he have personal integrity or a moral code or a conscience."

All of this added up to a man who would do anything for money and whose loyalty was for sale to the highest bidder. Matt definitely had to talk to Bellows tomorrow.

But right now, Faith was still pale and looking a little green around the gills. So Matt got up and dashed into the kitchen. He returned with the eggs and toast.

"Here. Eat this before it gets any colder."

She shook her head. "I don't think—"

"You're about to pass out or throw up, I'm not sure which," Matt persisted. "But the best thing you can do is get some food into your stomach. What do you want to drink?"

She picked up her fork, a good sign.

"Orange juice it is, then." He took a glass and filled it from the orange juice dispenser and set it in front of her. She turned it up and drank half in one breath.

"You live here upstairs, right?"

"Yes, of course."

"Alone?"

"Yes," Faith said. She searched Matt's dark eyes. "Why?

"Can you get someone to stay with you?"

"No. I mean, there's no need. Glo is here until nine o'clock most evenings, and Valerio comes in at 4:00 a.m. I'm alone for barely seven hours." She laughed. "Sometimes I wish I could afford more staff. I'd love to sleep late one morning."

"Do you have an alarm system?"

"No." She frowned at him. "Do you think Rory is dangerous? I don't. He gets frustrated and angry, and I'd trust a rattlesnake before I'd trust him, but he wouldn't hurt me."

"You couldn't prove that by me, not after what I saw this evening." Matt glanced around the café, his mind racing. "I'll stay here tonight."

"What? No, you won't."

"In fact," he said, hoping he wasn't getting in over his head. Bellows's suggestion that he stay around town was perfect timing. "The construction job is on hold— problem with materials delivery. I'll stay here for a few days. I can give you an extra hand during the town hall meeting, and I'll feel better about your safety."

He gauged her reaction and didn't like it. She was looking at him with suspicion clearly written all over her face. She was measuring him against Rory Stockett, and apparently, he was stacking up to be pretty much equal to the slick con man in her eyes.

But she had something else on her mind. "How do you know about the town hall meeting? It's not being announced until tomorrow morning."

Oops. Had he said that out loud? Matt hoped his expression stayed bland as he scrambled for an answer. "One of the guys I work with must have said something. He works at the Lockharts' ranch part-time."

Faith nodded, but the suspicion didn't fade from her eyes.

"Okay, then," Matt continued. "I'm going to sack out on one of those benches tonight. I'll leave your cook a note so when he comes in tomorrow he'll know I'm out here."

"I don't want you here," she said. "I don't need you."

"Look at me," he said. "You are in danger. I don't trust Stockett as far as I can throw him. If you don't let me stay here, I'm calling your cook or Glo and telling them to come in right now."

"Valerio has two children, boys, and Glo has cats."

"Then it's settled."

Faith got up and went around the counter to the cash register. She took a key out of her pocket and locked the drawer. When she saw him watching her, she blushed. "I do that every night," she said.

Matt nodded. "I'll get the lights."

For a second, she stood there as if she didn't know what to do. Matt understood. He had interrupted her routine. To be fair, Stockett had interrupted it first, but Matt had aided in the disruption.

Then she turned toward the stairs leading up to her

apartment. As she stepped on the first step, she uttered a little gasp, and her right hand went to her side.

"Faith, are you okay?"

She took a couple of short breaths. "Yes, I'm fine. Just Li'l Bit letting me know it's time for bed."

"You said *she* a while ago. You're having a girl?"

She glanced back at him over her shoulder. "I don't know—not officially. I haven't asked the sex of the baby but yes. I'm sure it's a girl."

Matt smiled. He could still remember when his twin sisters were born. He'd been thirteen, and he'd often babysat them while his mother worked. He'd loved playing with them, especially as they got old enough to toddle around. He made a game out of dressing them and trimming their hair differently, to see if his mother could still tell them apart. She always could.

His friends gave him hell about playing with dolls, but he didn't care. They were his baby sisters, and although he was only thirteen, he was man of the house and therefore responsible for keeping them safe and happy. "Have you thought of a name for her yet?"

Faith's mouth turned up in a smile, and she met his gaze. But then the smile faded and her back stiffened. "I have to get to bed," she said coolly. "Good night."

Matt watched her until her legs disappeared at the top of the stairs. He double-checked the front and back doors and the door to the basement, then he turned out the overhead lights and lay down, searching for a comfortable position on a bench that was several inches too short for his long legs.

Once again, Faith's attitude had changed midconversation. He'd asked one too many personal questions, gotten a little too close. Faith didn't trust him, and her attitude wasn't going to change anytime soon.

He had Rory Stockett to thank for that.

Chapter Four

Matt came awake instantaneously but didn't move a muscle. It was a skill he'd learned in combat in Iraq. He tried to identify the sound that had woken him but couldn't. Then he felt a presence standing over him.

He opened his eyes to see a hefty middle-aged man with slick black hair, a brown weathered face and an air force tattoo on his left bicep. He had on a white T-shirt and a white apron.

Matt moved to sit up, groaning internally at the pain of his stiff muscles. Sleeping curled up on the diner bench all night had been no picnic.

"No se mueva!"

Matt froze. "It's okay," he said. "I'm—"

"Matteo Soarez!" the man spat out, holding up the note Matt had left in the kitchen last night. *"Por qué estás aquí?"*

"Hey, buddy. *Hablo Inglés.*"

The man smiled, but on him it wasn't a nice expression. "So do I. What are you doing here?"

Matt slowly moved into a sitting position. "I'm here to protect Faith."

"And does she know about this?"

Matt yawned as he nodded. "Mind if I stand? It's

Valerio, right?" he asked, using the name he'd heard Faith use the night before.

In answer, Valerio backed away a couple of steps.

Matt stood, stretching out his legs and back. In some ways, sleeping on that cramped bench had been worse than sleeping on the ground in an airless tent in the desert.

"Thanks," he said. "I decided it would be best for me to sleep here after Rory Stockett came in just as Faith was trying to close."

At hearing Rory's name, Valerio spewed out a string of Spanish that should have turned the air blue.

"That's the impression I got, too," Matt said with a smile. "He tried to rough-handle Faith, so I stepped in."

For the first time, Matt saw a spark of interest and maybe even respect in Valerio's eyes. "Yeah? I don't see any blood."

"No blood, but Mr. Stockett is nursing a sore throat this morning."

Valerio nodded his approval. "And *mi ave blanca?*"

My white bird. A nice pet name for Faith. "She's upstairs, hopefully still asleep."

"Good." Valerio eyed Matt for a split second then jerked a thumb back toward the kitchen. "I'd better get started on the rolls and the chicken stock and heat up the grill for breakfast." He headed toward the door to the kitchen, then turned around.

"You know," he said. "If you're going to stay here, you're going to need a better place than a booth."

Matt arched his neck and winced. "Yeah," he said. "You're right about that."

Within an hour, the café was buzzing with activity

and gossip. Apparently the announcement of the governor's town hall meeting in Freedom had run on the early morning TV and radio shows, because everybody who came in for breakfast was talking about it.

Sheriff Hale didn't get a peaceful bite of breakfast for all the questions, most of which he couldn't answer. "First I heard about it was on the news this morning, too," he said over and over again.

His breakfast buddy Mayor Arkwright claimed not to know anything either, but unlike the sheriff, the mayor was full of opinions, and Matt thought it was a good thing Arkwright didn't get paid by the word.

"Well, if you were to ask me, my considered opinion is that our governor is making a grave error in holding an event of any kind here in Freedom so soon after the terrible tragedy of the Fourth of July parade." He barely paused to take a breath. "What I mean is that we all know the violence and bloodshed was supposedly directed at her daughter, but how can Governor Lockhart be certain of that? If she were to ask me, I'd advise her to stay out of the public eye for a period of time—that is, if she knows what's good for her."

As the mayor continued, a tall, attractive redhead came in to get a cup of coffee and a bagel. She sat at the counter next to Matt while she waited. "So you must be new around here," she said.

Matt nodded. "I've been here a little over a week."

"My name's Charlotte, Charlotte Manning."

"Matt Soarez."

Charlotte held his gaze and nodded. "Well, Matt Soarez, what brings you here?"

"Construction job," Matt said noncommittally.

Charlotte's eyes looked him up and down. "How long will you be in town?"

"Charlotte," Fred March interrupted.

Then Stan Lorry said, "Good to see you. I thought maybe you'd given up coffee."

Charlotte twirled on her bar stool. "Not at all, Fred. I'm just getting over a bad sinus infection. I've been sipping tea and taking cold medicine."

"Come sit with us for a minute," Stan invited her. "Tell us what you think about Lila's latest shenanigans. Seems like she'd figure she's done enough damage to Freedom already. People are just getting over the Fourth of July fiasco, and now she wants to hold a town hall meeting?"

Fred March chimed in. "One of these days Lila's going to push too far, and then we'd better all take a step back and watch out for the fireworks."

Glo appeared from the kitchen in time to hear the end of Fred's statement. "Aw, Fred, put a sock in it. The rest of you, too." She cocked an eyebrow at the mayor. Apparently Glo wasn't afraid of anybody.

"Has there ever been a governor you actually liked, Fred?" she snapped. "Or you, Stan?" She poured coffee all around before she continued.

"And if you think that blowhard Davidson on the radio has anything remotely intelligent to say, then I'll have to adjust my opinion of *your* IQ downward even farther." She set the coffeepot down, took a dish towel that was draped over one shoulder and started wiping down the counter.

"Stop for a minute and listen to yourselves. I'm not saying it, but some of what I'm hearing comes real close to sounding like a threat."

"Aw, give it a rest, Glo. We got a right to free speech, just like you do," Stan groused.

"Well, when you've got the governor's bodyguards around, not to mention maybe some feds, you're going to find out how they feel about the kind of free speech you folks are spreading around."

MATT LEFT THE CAFÉ EARLY, before Faith came downstairs. He went back to his apartment, took a shower and changed clothes. Then he called Bellows.

"I was just about to call you," Bellows said as soon as he picked up the phone. "I'm meeting with Gavin Farraday this morning. He's the governor's bodyguard in charge of security for the town hall meeting. He flew in late last night from Austin. He'll be here at 9:00 a.m. sharp. I want you here, too."

Matt dressed in pressed khaki slacks and a yellow polo shirt and drove to Bellows's mansion. He was ushered into the same room he'd been in before, where Bellows sat in his wheelchair behind the massive desk.

A medium-height man in a suit and tie with sharp features and sharper eyes rose from a leather sofa and held out his hand.

Bellows made the introductions, and Matt shook Farraday's hand briefly, then sat.

Bellows nodded to Farraday, who took up the conversation as if he hadn't been interrupted by the introductions. "We will have three bodyguards besides me. I and one other guard will be on stage with the governor. The other two will be in front of the podium, to thwart immediate attacks, if any." He looked at Matt. "What I need from you, Soarez, is your plan for utilizing the sheriff and his deputies and the three police officers from Amarillo."

Matt nodded and sat forward. "I outlined this for Mr. Bellows the other day, but I've refined it a bit since then. There needs to be two policemen at the front door and one at the back door that leads from the kitchen into the alley. Barricade the door to the basement and the stairs leading up to Faith's—Ms. Scott's—apartment. The sheriff and three of his deputies will remain outside to monitor the onlookers and to be ready in case someone runs. His other two men will control the media." Matt paused to take a breath.

"Whoever is after Governor Lockhart won't be interested in hurting innocent people," he said, "although he won't balk if he's cornered. He's probably working alone and will only have time to hit and run."

Farraday's expression barely changed, but Matt could tell the bodyguard liked what he'd heard. "And you?" he asked. "What will you be doing?"

"I'd prefer to be on the stage with the governor," Matt said. "I want to face the audience. I'll be looking for any suspicious body language, expressions or reactions." He spread his hands.

Farraday's gaze shifted from Matt to Bellows, and he gave a brief nod. Then he stood and held his hand out to Matt again.

"I've made arrangements to have communications devices and tasers transported to the Amarillo airport. They should be there by two o'clock this afternoon. Can you pick them up?"

Matt nodded. "Of course."

"Bring them here. We'll store them until Saturday," Bellows said.

Farraday nodded. "My team will pick them up on Saturday morning and bring them to the sheriff's office. We'll have enough for each deputy and each policeman. We'd like to meet with all of you Saturday morning."

"I'll let Sheriff Hale know."

"Good. I'll be in contact with you before then, Soarez. You and I will meet at least one more time prior to Saturday."

Matt shook Farraday's hand again. "Thank you, sir."

Once the bodyguard was gone, Matt turned to Bellows. "Do you have a minute, sir?"

"What's up?" Bellows asked in his no-nonsense way.

"There was an incident last night at the Talk of the Town Café."

Bellows's eyebrows went up.

"The father of Faith's baby, Rory Stockett, showed up and tried to bully her into giving him money. Luckily I was there. I warned Stockett not to bother her again. He threatened both of us."

"Stockett," Bellows said, frowning.

"First name Rory. Have you heard of him, sir?"

"I'm not sure. The name sounds familiar. It's possible I heard some gossip, and I'm thinking it was in connection with something illegal. Let me look into it. Do you have reason to think he might be connected to the threats against the governor?"

"Nothing concrete," Matt said. "But Faith—Ms. Scott—told me she hasn't seen him since she loaned him five thousand dollars six months ago. It seems a little coincidental that he would show up now, a couple of days before the governor's town hall meeting."

Bellows nodded. "It's worth looking into. I'll get someone on that. Anything else?"

"No, sir." Matt turned toward the door, then paused. "Actually there is one other thing. I'm moving into the café. I'll sleep on the floor if necessary, but I don't want to take the chance that Stockett will try to contact her again. Even if he's not connected to the threats, he could disrupt the meeting."

"That's up to you. You're not required to give me a blow by blow of where you are at any given time as long as you have your cell phone and I can get in touch with you. You do whatever you deem necessary to keep the governor safe and the town unharmed."

FAITH LIKED MID-AFTERNOONS at the café. The lunch crowd was gone by two, and they didn't start serving dinner until five o'clock. Not many people came in between two and five. Once in a while someone would show up for an afternoon piece of pie and coffee, and the mayor occasionally held afternoon meetings there, but usually the diner was quiet for three hours.

The kitchen ran like clockwork as long as Valerio was there. He had the preparations for dinner down to a science. Faith had made the pies this morning while Glo and Valerio handled the breakfast crowd.

By the time she'd come downstairs, Matt was gone. She didn't want to admit it—even to herself—but she was disappointed. She'd tried to convince him that he didn't need to spend the night in the restaurant, but with him downstairs, she'd slept better than she had since Gram died.

She sat at a table near the window, sipping a cup of herbal tea and folding flatware into snowy white napkins for the tables. She'd continued using cloth napkins after Gram died, although everybody encouraged her to change to paper. But she could hear Gram now.

No decent meal should be served with paper napkins.

The bell over the door rang, and a musical voice said, "Hi, Faith."

"Hi, Molly. Welcome back." Faith smiled at the teenager who worked as a bus girl and sometimes waitress at the café. Hiring Molly after she'd found out she was pregnant had turned out to be the smartest thing Faith had done in a long while.

Molly was trying to save up enough money to go to culinary school, and she was happy for the chance to observe and occasionally work with Valerio in the kitchen.

"Thanks. And thanks for the extra day off."

"Did your friend get moved?"

"Yes ma'am. And I'm ready to work the weekend." Molly jerked a thumb toward the window. "Or is that help wanted sign supposed to be a hint?"

Faith smiled. "Not at all, Molly. I don't know how we'd make it without you. I'm just making plans for the fall, when you leave to go to culinary school."

"Good," Molly said, making a show of wiping imaginary sweat from her brow. "I'll take any overtime you've got, too. I'm going to need the money."

"I'll take you up on the overtime," Faith said, "because this weekend is going to be busy. The governor is—"

"Going to have a town hall meeting. I know!" Molly grinned. "I am so excited. Have you seen her bodyguards? Some of them are hot!"

"You think they're hot? Wait til you see Matt Soarez," Faith murmured.

"Ma'am?"

Faith shook her head. "Nothing."

"Should I finish doing the setups?"

"No. I'd rather you help Valerio in the kitchen. You can cut the pies and get the bread baskets ready. I'm going to sit here and finish this."

"Okay."

"Molly? When you're done, ask Valerio to show you how to cut up a chicken for frying."

"I will. Thanks, Faith." Molly headed for the kitchen with a bounce in her step that Faith remembered having herself not so long ago.

"I don't bounce as much as I waddle now, do I Li'l Bit?" she whispered, folding a napkin and rolling a knife, fork and teaspoon inside, then securing the bundle with gummed paper.

As if in answer, a pain stabbed her on the right side of her tummy. She rubbed it. "Stop that, Li'l Bit. Why don't you take a nap?"

But the pain continued until Faith was taking short shallow breaths, trying not to trigger the squeezing pain. The pain went on for several minutes and then died down.

Faith turned and looked at the calendar that hung behind the cash register. She had a doctor's appointment on Monday. If this didn't get better, she'd tell the doctor and let him figure out what was the matter.

By five o'clock, the pain had diminished, so Faith acted as hostess and seated customers, talking with the regulars and reciting the specials and desserts to the others.

She didn't have a chance to relax until around eight o'clock, when most of the diners had cleared out. She realized she'd been watching the door all evening, but Matt hadn't shown up. It was unusual for him not to come in for a late dinner.

Why wasn't he here by now? A sinking dread settled in her chest. He'd come to town for a construction job. The first time Faith had seen him was seven—no eight—days ago. Was the job done? Was he not coming back?

She shook her head at that thought. He wouldn't leave without telling her, would he? Especially since he'd offered to sleep here to protect her from Rory.

Even as she asked herself that question, she knew she was being naive.

Matt Soarez had no obligation whatsoever to inform her of his plans. He'd stepped forward like a knight in shining armor to defend her against Rory's rough handling, but any man worth his salt would have done the same.

Maybe because of the fight he'd forgotten to mention that his job here was done.

With a sigh and a conscious effort to keep silly tears from forming in her eyes, Faith went to the cash register and got out the credit card receipts. There were no customers lingering this evening, so she could go ahead and start verifying them. Maybe tonight she could get upstairs to bed before ten.

She was bent over the pile of receipts when the bell over the door rang. Her head flew up like a shot—maybe it was Matt. But no.

The man standing inside the door was medium height and big all over, like a linebacker. His head was shaven, and his broad face sported a nose that appeared to have been broken more than once. He wore a dark suit that fit him well, even across his massive shoulders, with a white shirt and a school tie. He shot his cuffs and smoothed his tie as his gaze slid around the room.

Apparently satisfied that there was no one in the dining room but Faith, he walked over to the counter and placed his considerable bulk on a stool.

"Coffee," he muttered. He unbuttoned his jacket and let it hang open, allowing Faith a glimpse of steel. Her pulse jumped. He had a gun. A part of her brain wondered why he bothered. He didn't look like he needed any extra weaponry.

Her throat went dry. "R-regular or decaf?" she croaked. The man frowned at her. "Coffee," he growled.

Faith grabbed a mug, squeezing it to keep her fingers from shaking, poured him a cup and set it down in front of him.

"Would you like sugar or cre—"

The man wrapped a nearly unbelievably large hand around her wrist.

She jerked away, shocked. Of course jerking did absolutely no good. The man tightened his grip, and she felt her fingers tingle. He was cutting off the circulation.

"Did you forget that your loan's due, Ms. Scott?" he asked softly.

She couldn't comprehend what he was saying. "My what?"

"Your loan, sugar. Five large."

"L-large?"

The man's mouth twisted into a grimace, and he huffed a couple of times. His version of a chuckle?

"Five thousand dollars," he said slowly, as if to a child.

"I don't—" Faith shook her head "—I don't know what you're talking about."

He let go of her wrist, and she shook her hand. The blood rushing back into her fingers made them prick as if needles were jabbing them.

"Don't act like an idiot, sugar. You took out a loan six months ago."

Six months ago. Of course. Her heart sank to her toes, and her breath grew short. "Rory—my…my ex-fiancé. He got—he's the one who took out the loan. He's paying it off," she paused, a sick sinking feeling pressing down on her chest. "Isn't he?"

The big man shook his head and made that awful face and noise that must be his version of a laugh. "You talking about Stockett?" His shoulders shook.

"Oh, sugar." The man shook his head back and forth, back and forth, then eyed her tummy. "I'm afraid your boyfriend screwed you twice."

Faith's heart jumped into her throat and lodged there. "Oh, no," she mouthed. "Oh, no."

"Oh, yes. When Stockett took out the loan, he made arrangements to pay it off in six months. That six months is up today. He gave us this address."

"Oh, my God," Faith whispered. Of course Rory would run off and leave her with the debt on the loan. She'd thought she couldn't be any more of an idiot than to give Rory money borrowed against her café. But the man was right. Rory had definitely screwed her twice.

"How—how much do I owe?" she asked, feeling her shoulders slump in defeat. "I'll need to make arrangements to pay it off over time."

The big man sent her a look that almost appeared to have regret in it. "Sugar," he said, "you don't have no idea, do you?"

That expression on his broad face and those regretful words frightened her more than anything he'd done yet. "What do you mean?" she croaked.

"My boss is in the business of loaning money to people who can't get a loan through the usual channels. Our terms are hundred percent interest, payable at the end of the agreed-upon time. For you, sugar, that means you owe ten thousand as of today. If you can't pay today, well, my boss don't accept 'can't pay.' He also don't accept 'more time.' You need to get the money somehow." He looked around. "You got any insurance on this place?"

Faith was too shocked to even react. Her eyes burned, her head spun, but all she could do was stand there and stare at the man. "Insurance?" she repeated stupidly.

"Yeah. On the café. On the building."

She nodded, not quite sure what he was asking.

"How much?"

Faith swallowed and felt the blood drain from her face. Her head started to pound.

"Come on, sugar. Don't faint on me. How much?"

"One hun—" she took a shuddering breath "—one hundred thousand."

At her reply, the man shook his head. "Damn, sugar. You can't rebuild this place for a hundred thou. But what you can do is this. If you can't come up with ten large by Sunday, your place here will burn down. Then you can collect the insurance and pay off your debt."

"But this was my grandmother's café. Her home. It's all I have."

"Sugar, after you pay us off, you'll have ninety thousand."

Faith felt a lump lodge in her throat. This was Gram's café, her pride and joy. She'd told Faith ever since she was a little girl that the café would be hers.

She clenched her jaw to stop the tears that were threatening to crawl up the back of her throat. What could she do? Rory had left her with nothing—no choice. All the promises he'd made and he hadn't meant a single one.

The man stood, adjusted his jacket so his gun didn't show, tossed a bill on the counter and gave her one last look. "I'll check with you Sunday."

As the big man left the café, Faith's whole body began to tremble, and she couldn't draw a full breath into her constricted chest. She panted shallowly, her lungs straining for air. But the more she tried, the more panicked she became.

She tented her hands over her mouth, hoping that would help her to breathe normally, but fear had taken over her body. She could never raise ten thousand dollars in two years, much less two days.

She was going to lose everything.

Chapter Five

A WWE-sized guy in a dark suit was getting into a black Land Rover just as Matt pulled in to the Talk of the Town Café parking lot. The sight tripped Matt's internal warning system. When the man started the vehicle, the license plate light came on, and Matt noted and memorized the number.

Two things struck him as odd. Nobody, not even the mayor, wore a suit here in the summer. It was too damn hot. And muscle heads in expensive suits and expensive cars didn't eat in small town cafés—ever.

When Matt stepped inside and saw Faith, her face was white as a sheet and her hands were wrapped protectively around her tummy.

"Faith," he said, going to her. "What's the matter?"

She looked up at him, her face a mask of fear. She opened her mouth, but nothing came out. All she could do was shake her head.

He sat down next to her and took her hands in his. They were cold as ice and trembling. "Faith?"

At that instant, Glo came out of the kitchen, carrying a tray of newly washed mugs. "What's going on out here?" she asked. "From the way the bell kept ringing, I thought we were having a late rush."

Matt didn't speak. He held Faith's gaze. She didn't move a muscle, but somehow he knew that she didn't want Glo to know about whatever had happened. And whatever it was, it was directly related to the big man who'd just left the café.

Glo turned to Faith. "You all right, honey?"

"Sure," she said. "I'm fine. Just hurting a little." She pulled her hands away from Matt's and rubbed the side of her tummy. "Aren't you done yet? I thought you'd already left to go home. I told you, I don't want you wearing yourself out before I even go to the hospital."

Glo's eyes narrowed as she assessed Faith, then she turned, taking the opportunity to glare at Matt before heading back into the kitchen. He got her unspoken message. *You will tell me what's going on.*

Once they were alone again, Faith clasped her hands together. "I—I need to talk to you."

"Okay. Want to sit over there? I'll bring you a glass of water, and you tell me what's got you so spooked."

"No," she said quickly. "I mean, can we go upstairs? I don't want anybody to hear."

"Sure," he said. He couldn't quite figure out what was wrong with her, but he knew one thing for certain. It had something to do with the hulking wrestler wannabe who had just left.

Faith took it slowly up the stairs. Behind her, Matt watched her hand grip the stair rail until the skin over her knuckles looked transparent. She managed to make it up the steps without pausing, but once they were at the top landing, she sighed deeply.

"Here we are," she said, trying hard to keep her breathing steady, although it was clear to Matt that she was winded.

"What does your doctor say about you climbing stairs?"

She avoided his gaze as she took a set of keys out of her pocket and opened the door to her apartment.

"Who has keys to the café and your apartment?" he asked.

"Glo has a master key, like I do." She looked at her key ring. "And there's a key to the diner's front and back doors hanging in the kitchen." She separated out a key and slid it off the ring. "This is another master key. It opens all the doors in the building. Maybe you should take one, since you're probably going to be in and out at all hours of the day and night."

Matt accepted the key and slipped it onto his key ring. Then he stepped inside. The apartment was large and bright. The living room was about half the size of the dining room below, and to his left were two bedrooms, divided by a central bath. Matt could see a big four-poster bed in the larger bedroom, which looked to be the same size as the living room. The smaller room was covered with plastic, and several paint cans sat on the floor. The kitchen was to the right, which put it above the diner's kitchen.

The apartment looked like Faith. The windows faced north. During the day, they'd provide that pure, indirect light that painters love so much. The sheer curtains matched the glow in Faith's cheeks. There were blinds, but it didn't look like she lowered them very often. The rug picked up the blue of her eyes.

The living room furniture was old, and the upholstery was faded—her grandmother's, he guessed. In the southwest corner sat a rocking chair with a pink-and-blue afghan draped over it. The effect was charming, pretty and sweet, just like her.

"I see you're working on your nursery," he said, gesturing toward the unfinished room. "And you already have a rocking chair."

"I'd hoped to be finished painting it by now," Faith said, her voice unsteady. "But it's been so busy." She stopped.

Matt turned. Had he upset her? Because she was definitely on the verge of tears. She'd crossed her arms, hugging herself, and her face had taken on a greenish tinge. "Yeah, hon?" He stepped toward her.

"I'm so sorry, but—" she stopped and pressed her lips together.

"Faith?"

Suddenly she looked terrified. He stepped closer.

Her face crumpled and tears started to flow. She covered her face with her hands and mumbled something that was too muffled to understand.

Matt couldn't figure out what had caused her to cry, but he knew he couldn't stand there and do nothing. He reached out and touched the curve of her shoulder. When he did, she leaned toward him. In a motion as natural as breathing, Matt held out his arms, and Faith stepped into them. She pressed her face against his shirt and sobbed.

He put his arms around her in a comforting gesture, but as his shirt grew damp with her tears, he clenched his jaw. Holding Faith as she cried was anything but comfortable for him. Her body against his stirred a reaction in him that he'd done his best to pretend wasn't there.

"Shh," he whispered, keeping his frustration out of his voice. "Everything's going to be okay. Don't worry."

"I'm sorry," she mumbled without lifting her head.

He cupped the back of her head, feeling her silky hair against the sensitive skin of his palm. "Shh. Just calm down, and tell me what's wrong."

"I feel so stupid. I don't know what to do." Her voice broke off.

"I'll be glad to help you with anything, Faith. No matter what. If it's getting the nursery painted, or—"

She shook her head. "No, you won't want to help. Not when you hear what it is." She pushed against his chest, so he relented and let her step away. "But you don't have to get involved. I just need some information. Maybe you can tell me if you know someone I can call, or—"

"Faith, here." He took her hands lightly in his, barely even a touch. "Sit. Where do you like to sit? In that armchair or in the rocker?"

"Rocker," she muttered.

"Okay, then." He led her to the rocking chair. Once she was seated, he went into the kitchen, found a glass and filled it with water. Faith took the glass and drank thirstily.

"Now talk to me." He sat gingerly on the edge of her couch. He didn't want to get too comfortable in her apartment. He'd be done with this assignment before long, and there would be no excuse for him to stay around Freedom, much less around Faith's apartment.

"First, tell me why you don't want Valerio and Glo to know that there's anything wrong. Not that you've fooled them. Glo knows something's up, and from the look she gave me, she thinks it's my fault." He gave her a little smile.

But she didn't smile back. She looked miserable, and the fear hadn't disappeared from her eyes.

"This is about that man in the suit, isn't it?"

She looked up, startled, then nodded. "You saw him?"

"Who is he?"

"I swear, Matt. I don't know."

"Okay. What did he want?"

"I told you Rory asked me for money."

Matt nodded. "Boy meets girl, et cetera."

"Well, Rory put me in touch with a friend of his who could set up a loan with a decent interest rate." She stopped and uttered a harsh little sound that might have been a laugh. "And he promised he'd pay it back—that it was his debt and I wouldn't be bothered by anyone."

Matt leaned forward and put his elbows on his knees. He looked at his clasped hands rather than at Faith. People were scammed like this all the time. Everybody knew the stories. He'd have hoped Faith would be smarter than to believe Stockett's lies.

"Well, it was a decent rate, all right—for Rory," she said bitterly. Her bottom lip started to tremble. "That man told me—he told me—that the five thousand dollars had gone up to ten thousand, and..." A sob interrupted her. Then another. She couldn't go on.

Matt shot up off the bed and walked over to the window, which looked out onto the parking lot behind Talk of the Town Café.

Damn it. Stockett had set Faith up with a loan shark. If he could get his hands on the slick grifter, he'd—

"Matt?" Faith's voice sounded small and scared.

He turned around. "Okay, what did he say he would do?"

"He asked me if I had insurance on the café, and I told him I did. A hundred thousand. He said if I couldn't come up with the ten thousand by Sunday, the café would burn and I'd collect the insurance. I could pay them and keep the rest." She stopped and put her hands over her mouth. "Gram left this café to me. It's all I have. And now I'm going to lose it." She sniffed. "How could I have been so stupid?"

Matt went over to her, bent down and took her hands in his. "Listen to me, Faith. Is there anything you have that you could liquidate to give them at least part of their payment?"

"I don't—wait!" A tad of color blushed across her cheeks. "Rory gave me an engagement ring. I didn't throw it away or give it back to him. I thought he owed me something for my baby. I was saving it for her."

Matt had a feeling he knew what Faith was going to show him, but he smiled and nodded encouragingly. "Get it, and let's take a look."

Faith went to her closet and dug around for a few seconds in the back and then came up with the ring. Matt was no expert at diamonds, but he knew how to tell if one was real. Diamonds were the hardest natural substance. He took the ring from her and took out his pocketknife.

"What are you doing?"

"Trust me, Faith. If this ring is worth anything, my knife can't hurt it."

Her face fell. "It's fake, isn't it? Somehow, I'm not surprised."

Matt turned on her bedside table lamp and looked closely at the ring. It was a marquis cut solitaire. On its face, it was beautiful. He inspected the inside of the band. Nothing was stamped there. He turned it upside down and scraped the underside of the stone. Sure enough, the knife left a mark. Then he scraped the inside of the gold band that held the diamond. Minuscule flecks of gold appeared on the tip of his knife, leaving silver scratches on the surface of the band.

He looked up. "I'm sorry."

She shrugged, and it was clear that she was devastated. "What else should I expect from a man like him?"

Taking the ring back, she slid it onto her finger and stared at it, as if remembering the night Rory had given it to her. Then she tugged it off and tossed it toward a trash can. It missed and bounced on the hardwood floor. "So much for saving the café," she said wryly.

"Don't give up yet," Matt said. "You own the café free and clear, right?"

"Except for that stupid loan," she answered.

"Give me a little while. I'll bet I can figure something out. What kind of papers did you sign?" he asked.

"I'll get them."

Matt looked at his watch. "Tell you what. You find them for me. Then you get back to work on the town hall meeting. Forget about the guy in the suit. I'll see you later."

"Matt?"

He looked up as Faith stepped closer to him. She lay a hand on his arm. "Thank you," she said softly.

Her lips were parted and her eyes, still sparkling with tears, seemed to be asking him a silent question.

Matt wanted to back away. Okay, *wanted* was probably not the right word. He *needed* to back away, for both their sakes. But he couldn't. He was held there, mesmerized by her blue eyes. He covered her hand with his and then leaned down and kissed her softly.

To his amazement and delight, she kissed him back. Then the amazement and delight changed to something sweeter and sharper than anything he'd ever felt before. He moved in closer, turning the kiss from sweet to sexy. Faith followed where he led.

But suddenly she pulled away.

"No," she muttered. "No, no, no."

"Faith?" Matt was left with an uncomfortable tightness in his jeans and a sense of bewilderment.

She put a hand to her mouth and avoided his gaze. "I—I have to—you know—get some sleep. I have to be up early."

Matt backed toward the door. "Right," he said, hoping his face wasn't as red as it felt. "I need to go, too. I'll let you know what I find out."

How many ways could she come up with to screw up her life? Faith thought as she splashed water on her face, hoping to erase the traces of tears—and of Matt's kiss.

For an instant, she allowed herself to relive that moment of bliss when their lips met. Something had happened to her in that tiny space of time. It wasn't just a kiss—not for her. It was a promise, filled with strength and hope. Matt Soarez was a man worthy of trust.

As soon as the thought formed in her head, she banished it. *No.* He wasn't trustworthy. He was an itinerant worker—a drifter, just like Rory. And just like Rory he'd be gone in a flash.

A lump rose in her throat as she thought of Rory. She'd believed he really loved her. She'd accepted his ring with trust and love. She hadn't intended to get pregnant, but Rory had seemed thrilled. So she'd begun to think of them as a family: Rory, the baby and her.

Then Rory started talking about buying a big rig and starting a trucking business. It would bring in good money, he'd told her. Eventually, he'd worn her down with his optimism and confidence.

She'd agreed to take out a loan against her café, and Rory had agreed to pay it off. But as soon as he had the money, he was gone, leaving her devastated.

But now she'd lived with the baby inside her for eight months. Carrying her child had given her inner strength and confidence in herself. She knew that she and her baby would be just fine alone.

Faith rubbed her tummy. "Right, Li'l Bit?" she asked. "We can work together. Here's what I need you to do. If I *ever* start thinking that I could have a future with Matt, you've got to kick me. Agreed?"

To her surprise, a quick, sharp pain in her side gave her the baby's answer.

"Ouch," she said. "That was good. Maybe not so hard, though."

As THEY PREPARED FOR the dinner crowd the next evening, Faith asked Glo what she thought about Matt.

"Here's what I think," Glo said, propping her fists on her hips. "I think you need to tell me what was going on last night."

"Going on?" Faith repeated. "What do you mean?"

"Now you listen to me, girlie. I'll go to Matt and get the information out of him if you don't tell me. And I mean right *now!*"

"Nothing was going on," Faith lied. She didn't want

Glo worrying about the loan. Plus, as good-hearted and loyal as Glo was, she did like to gossip, so news of Faith's stupidity would travel like wildfire.

"Faith, honey, you know better than to lie to me," the older woman said with a smirk as she studied Faith's face for a few seconds. Then she shook out her apron, tied it around her waist and patted her hair. "Seems to me that you two are getting awfully chummy. Could it be there's a mutual attraction growing?"

"Glo, please," Faith said, trying to pretend her cheeks weren't heating up. "I don't have time to listen to your fantasizing. I merely wondered if you think we can trust him."

"Fantasizing? Is that what it is? You don't think I've noticed that he's here every single minute these days? You don't think everybody in town has started to notice how he's hanging around?"

Faith frowned. Was Glo right? "Well, everybody can just stop worrying. I'm not going to be fooled by a drifter ever again, Glo. I mean look at him. Could he be any more exactly like Rory?"

Glo brushed her hands down her bright green apron and checked to make sure her order pad was in her pocket. "Like Rory? Come on, Faith. There's no comparison. Rory was so slick he practically oozed. You ask me, Matt Soarez is the genuine article. I'd trust a man in faded jeans and work boots all day long up against a slick piece of work in dress pants and ridiculous loafers with fringe and little bow ties."

"But Matt's only here for a construction job. He'll be gone in a flash, as soon as the job is over." A pang zinged her in the middle of her chest at that thought.

"Not to mention that the last thing I need is another con man without two dimes to rub together."

"Honey, I know Rory broke your heart. That was the first time you'd ever been in love, but you mark my words. You could do a hell of a lot worse than Matt Soarez. And—" Glo sent a knowing glance at Faith's tummy "—you're going to find out it's damned hard to raise a kid alone."

Faith walked around the counter and unlocked the cash register. "You don't have to tell me that, Glo. I'm aware."

Glo patted her blond hair as the bell over the door rang, announcing the first of the dinner customers. "By the way. Deputy Appleton told me he saw Rory the other evening. He didn't come here, did he?"

Faith avoided Glo's gaze.

"So he did. You watch out, honey. Don't get tangled up with him again."

"Don't worry," Faith said. "I don't intend to."

"Good. And Faith—"

Faith smiled wryly. There was no end to Glo's advice, once she got started.

"Matt's staying here to protect you. How long are you going to make him sleep down here in a cramped little booth that's a foot too short for him?" With that, Glo nodded at the couple who'd just come in and grabbed the coffeepot.

Chapter Six

After Matt left Faith, he'd driven to Amarillo to the airport to pick up the equipment that Gavin Farrady had sent. While he was there, he ran by the house he'd rented for his mother as soon as he'd taken the job from Bart Bellows. She was cooking, of course.

"Is everything okay, Matteo?" she asked him, tilting her head up for him to kiss her cheek. "I thought you said your job would keep you too busy to visit for a while."

"I'm busy, but since I was here in town I thought I'd come by and check on you."

Coredad Soarez narrowed her black eyes at her son. "Somehow I think there is more to this visit than a desire to see your mother."

Matt grabbed a hot empanada from the pan his mom had just taken out of the oven. He juggled it until it cooled, then bit into it. "I did want to ask you if you'd mind loaning the crib to someone who's about to have a baby."

"Someone?" His mom slid the rest of the empanadas off the baking sheet onto a plate, then turned around. "What someone?"

"Her name is Faith Scott. She owns a café, and she doesn't have a crib."

"And where is her husband?"

Matt studied the last bite of the empanada he held in his hand. "She doesn't have a husband either."

"Ah."

He winced. His mother's *ahs* could be a whole language unto themselves.

"Of course she may borrow the crib," she said. "It has held beautiful babies. You tell her that her child will be blessed."

"Thanks, Mom," Matt said, breathing a silent sigh of relief. He'd gotten off easy this time. "I'll load it into the pickup and get going. I've got to—"

"Oh, no," Coredad Soarez said. "You don't *got to* do nothing until you sit down and tell me all about this Faith Scott. How far along is she? Is she having a boy or a girl? Where's the father?"

It was another hour before Matt was able to head back toward Freedom. He was on his way to Bart Bellows's place to drop off the equipment when his phone rang.

It was Farraday. The governor's chief of security wanted to go over the plans for security at the town hall meeting on Saturday. He asked Matt to meet him at the Corps Security and Investigations headquarters. CSAI offices were just outside of Freedom in an old rifle factory that had been turned into office buildings. He didn't want to take a chance on them being seen together.

"Did you pick up the equipment?" Farraday asked as soon as they were inside the CSAI conference room.

"Yeah. This afternoon. I have it in the backseat of my truck, in the shipping boxes."

Farraday glanced out the window. "Is that your truck with the baby bed in the back? Are you sure our equipment is safe?"

"Has been so far. I just picked it up this morning."

"And you came straight here?"

"No. I went by my mother's house for a few minutes first."

"So you haven't had time to inventory it or test the equipment."

"Actually, I checked the boxes there at the airport when I signed for them. Then I stopped in the taxi parking lot and tested the com units. Sadly, I couldn't recruit any volunteers to test the tasers on, except myself. They worked on the lowest setting." Matt rubbed his left palm. "They worked well," he added.

"Okay." Farraday leaned forward, his elbows on the long mahogany conference table. "Governor Lockhart will arrive at the Talk of the Town Café at seven o'clock Saturday night. She'll be in a dark SUV. We'll bring her into the dining room through the kitchen door. We'll have a raised platform specially built to go behind the counter for the governor to stand on."

Matt nodded. "Do you need to do a walk-through of the café before Saturday?"

"No. I have a scale drawing. The platform's going to be necessarily small, because of the limited space behind the counter. The governor, myself, Mayor Arkwright and two other bodyguards will be there. Arkwright will step down and join the audience once he's finished with his introduction of the governor. You said you wanted to observe from the platform. So once Mayor Arkwright leaves, you can step up. You'll be closest to the door to the kitchen. Does that work for you?"

"Yeah. Sounds good."

"I have the scale drawing right here." Farraday spread the sheet out on the table between them. "Where are you and the sheriff planning to place the deputies?"

Matt went over and finalized the security plans with Farraday. Farraday nodded his approval.

"I do wish we had a more secure facility," Matt said.

"Me, too, but the café is what the governor wants." Farraday shrugged, a what-are-you-going-to-do gesture.

"Has anyone briefed Faith about her role in the meeting?"

"Faith?" Farraday looked puzzled. "Oh, Ms. Scott, the owner? The governor's PR person, Tanya Gossett, is talking with her."

"What's the time frame for the meeting?"

"The governor wants to speak for about twenty minutes, then open up the floor for questions. We plan to shut it down by nine o'clock. We'll take her out through the kitchen, just like she came in, and put her into the waiting SUV. Your guys will have to disperse the crowd."

"So realistically, what do you think is the likelihood of someone trying to harm the governor during the meeting?"

Farraday frowned. "I'm afraid the odds are increasing. Did Bart tell you about the note the governor received after the Fourth of July parade?"

Matt shook his head no.

"It was very short and to the point. It said *Time to die, Lila.*"

"How was it delivered?"

"It was in with her mail. Nobody knows how it got in there."

"What do you think?"

"I don't know," Farraday said. "It was printed in block letters on cheap copy paper. No envelope. They used her given name, but she's widely known as Lila, so that doesn't really tell us anything."

"Then we have to assume that she's in grave danger. Will she be wearing body armor?"

Farraday smiled wryly. "Not unless we wrestle her to the ground and force it on her. And that's not going to happen."

Matt was surprised. "Are you kidding? Because if she were under my protection, that's exactly what I'd do."

"Yeah? Well, obviously, you've never dealt with Governor Lila Lockhart."

JUST AS FAITH FINISHED verifying the credit card receipts late Thursday evening, Matt knocked on the front door. She ran to the door and unlocked it.

He smiled at her, and her heart gave a little leap. "I see you listened to me and locked up," he said, indicating the door.

Faith nodded. "I've just told my regulars that if they want pie after nine o'clock, they'll have to call first, so I'll know they're coming.

"Speaking of pie—" she chuckled "—I saved you a piece of the cherry. And let me tell you it wasn't easy. The mayor had to settle for apple."

"You're the best," he said, touching her chin with his forefinger.

Faith felt the touch all the way down to her toes. Just

as she was making a mental note to give herself another lecture about him, she felt a sharp pain in her side. The baby.

"Thanks," she murmured, aiming the remark at both Matt and her baby.

"So what's going on with the town hall meeting?" Matt asked casually.

Faith frowned at him. His tone was odd—almost *too* casual, as if he was forcing it. "Everything's on schedule, I think. The mayor's public relations assistant called today, and we went over their plans. It sounds like the governor's staff is on top of everything. They seem to have it running like a well-oiled machine."

"Good." He paused, and his gaze shifted around the room. "I've been contacted by a bodyguard for the governor to help with keeping an eye out for trouble-makers."

"Really? You?" Faith said, surprised. Immediately, she realized how her unthinking words sounded. "I didn't mean—"

Matt waved away her apology. "Apparently Mr. Bellows recommended a couple of us who're working on his driveway as muscle in case of any trouble. I told them I'd be glad to. I mean, I'll be here anyway."

For some reason, Faith's face grew warm. "I'd better get the cash register closed out. And you need your pie. Do you want ice cream with it?"

Matt nodded and sat on a stool. He pulled out a five dollar bill and laid it on the counter.

"Matt, please stop trying to pay for everything. You're staying here to…to protect me. I owe you much more than a few meals and some pie." Faith pulled out the piece of pie she'd saved for him and added a generous scoop of ice cream.

Matt didn't answer her. He just dug into the dessert.

As Faith finished closing out the register and locked it, she thought about what Glo had said this morning. "Matt?"

He was finishing up his pie. As he scraped the plate with his fork, he looked up at her.

"Would you..." she started. How was she going to ask him this without making it sound like a proposition? "Would you want to sleep upstairs? In the living room I mean. On the couch. In the living room." She took a deep breath. "You already have a key."

Matt had eaten the last dregs of the pie and ice cream. He laid the fork down beside the plate, then spent a few unnecessary seconds straightening it.

"That would be nice," he said finally. "The booths are great for sitting, but they're a little short and narrow for sleeping on."

Faith nodded. That had gone better than she'd expected it to. Once again, she was impressed at how open and genuine he was. Rory would have leered and made a suggestive remark, as would some other men in town. But Matt took the invitation for what it was and answered politely. Glo's words echoed in her ears.

Matt Soarez is the genuine article. I'd trust a man in faded jeans and work boots all day long.

"Okay, then," she said. "I'll go upstairs and get out some sheets and a quilt—for the couch."

"In the living room," Matt said with a smile.

THE NOISE STARTLED FAITH out of a deep sleep. For a split second, before she came completely awake, she thought it was part of a dream. Then something heavy hit the mattress, sending shock waves through her. Tiny pricks peppered her arms.

What was it? Ants? Still half asleep, she pushed the covers back. She had to get them off her.

Then she was blinded by sudden light.

"Faith! Don't move!"

She blinked in the brightness. It was Matt. He'd turned on the overhead light. His sharp eyes took in her bed and her in one glance.

"I don't know what happened," she gasped, looking down at herself. Her arms and gown and sheet were covered with sparkly glass. She lifted an arm to brush it away.

"Be still!" Matt yelled, flipping the lights off, then vaulting toward the window. He looked out.

"Matt? What is it?"

No answer. He hit a preset number on the phone he held. "Sheriff, someone just threw a brick through Faith's window. I saw a figure get into a dark pickup. I think he drove west." He paused. "Good. Both ends of the street. Thanks!"

"Matt, do something!" Faith cried. "Tell me something."

He stayed at the window for a few seconds, then turned and glanced at her, then at the door, as if debating whether to stay or go. He headed toward the door, but all he did was turn on the lights.

"Are you hurt?" he asked, his gaze roaming over her and the bed.

"I don't think so."

"Oh, God!" he breathed in a strangled voice.

"What?" Faith looked down at herself uncomprehendingly. But within a second or two, the sounds, the dots of pain like ant bites, Matt's words, all made sense. She was covered with tiny bits of glass. It glittered on her gown and arms and sparkled on her sheets. In the bright overhead light, she looked as if she was in a bizarre, gaudy painting.

Then she saw it—what Matt had seen. She opened her mouth but nothing came out. She couldn't get her breath.

A huge shard of glass—at least six inches long and sharp on both ends—had buried itself upright, like a sword, less than four inches from her left thigh. Just behind it, near her hip, was an old brick with a note attached to it by a rubber band.

Matt took a couple of quick pictures with the cell phone in his hand.

"What—what are you doing?"

"If anything comes up later, I want to be able to prove that this is more than just a prank. You could have been seriously hurt or killed."

Faith looked back at the lethal shard of glass. She tried to swallow, but her throat was too dry.

"Where are your shoes?" Matt asked, still staring at the shard.

"My—" Faith was having trouble processing what Matt was saying. Her heart was pounding in her ears, her mouth and throat were almost too dry to talk and her limbs had started trembling.

"There they are," he muttered. He picked up a pair of slides and clapped the soles together, then brushed them off with his fingers. He set them on the floor beside the bed.

"I want you to do exactly as I say, okay?"

She nodded.

"First of all, do not move a muscle unless I specifically tell you to. If there's another large piece of glass somewhere, you could cut or stab yourself."

He glanced around and spotted her robe. Grabbing it, he used it to pick up the brick. "The surface is probably too rough for fingerprints, but maybe we can get something from the note."

Then, with a sleeve of her robe around his hand, he grabbed the shard of glass like a knife and pulled on it.

To Faith's horror and dismay, Matt had a little difficulty extracting the shard from her mattress. She tried her best to wipe her mind of the picture that rose, a picture of that shard embedded in her thigh.

He laid the robe on her dresser.

Faith looked down at herself. She had on a long nightgown, but it had ridden up. Her hand reached out to tug it down.

"Faith!"

She froze. "I can't sit here without moving any longer," she said.

"Okay. Just a second. We've got to be careful." He inspected the sheet beside her hips and thighs. "Okay, sit up carefully. You've got broken glass all over you. Then turn sideways."

Faith did as she was told. She felt a couple of pricks on the backs of her knees.

"Now I'm going to put your shoes on for you, then you just stand straight up. Got it?" He knelt. His hands were large but amazingly gentle as he ran them around her ankles and over the top and sole of her foot before he slipped each sandal on.

Then he stood and held out his hand. She put her right hand in his.

"Stand up," he said and tugged. She stood. Glass pinged onto the hardwood floor. A few tiny bits hit the tops of her feet.

"Take a change of clothes into the bathroom and shower. Have you got flip-flops you can wear in the shower so you don't cut your feet?"

She nodded. "What about the brick? There's a note attached to it."

"I'm going to read it. Where's a broom and mop?"

"In the closet at the top of the stairs," she said as she headed to the bathroom.

Once she'd finished her shower and wiped out the tub with wet toilet paper, trying to clean out the last tiny pieces of glass, she came out of the bathroom to find Matt closing the bedroom door.

"I don't want to disturb the bed until the sheriff has had a chance to see and photograph it for evidence," he said.

Faith nodded, speechless. She was frozen by the sight before her. She'd been too terrified to notice him when he'd rushed into her room to find her covered with glass.

But now those few moments were crystal clear. He'd had on boxer shorts and a sleeveless undershirt. His tanned skin had gleamed. Then she'd been too frightened to react, but now, although at some point while she was showering he'd pulled on jeans, her brain zinged straight back to the sight of him dressed in nothing but his underwear.

Despite the fact that she'd been attacked in her bed and should be frightened out of her mind, at this moment her brain was filled with the sight of his muscled thighs, shoulders and biceps. And the dominant impression in her mind was that he'd have jumped in front of the brick or even the shards of glass if he could have.

She mentally shook her head. She had to get over this notion that Matt Soarez was much, much more than he seemed. She had no concrete reason to doubt that he was anything more than a construction worker, in town for a few days to finish up a job. But there was something wrong with that picture.

Matt, still searching the floor for bits of glass, spoke without looking up. "You should wear shoes around here for a while, until you're sure you've gotten up all the glass." He raised his head and his eyes widened.

She looked down at herself and saw what Matt saw. Minuscule beads of blood had popped out on her shoulders and arms. She swiped a finger across an itchy place on her cheek and looked at it. Sure enough there was a streak of blood staining her fingertip.

"Damn it, Faith," he said, with a look in his eyes that she'd never seen in any man's eyes before. It frightened and thrilled her at the same time. Matt was enraged, but not at her—for her. Some base instinct inside her responded to his primal reaction.

"I—I cleaned all the glass and put alcohol on the spots," she stammered.

He stood the broom against the wall and gently wrapped his fingers around her arm. He examined it closely, then looked up at her from beneath the longest, blackest eyelashes she'd ever seen.

"Are there worse cuts?" he asked in a quiet even voice that belied the dark expression on his face.

"No," she said. "This one," she said and pointed to a strip bandage at her shoulder, "is the worst."

He let go of her arm and spread his palm above her tummy, but stopped short of touching it. "The baby?"

Faith smiled. "Apparently she slept through the whole thing, although she's awake now." Then, following an instinct she didn't quite understand, she looked up at him. "Would you like to feel her?"

Matt didn't move his hands, so Faith laid her hand over his and guided it to her right side. "She kicks me here all the time."

She pressed his hand against her tummy. "I keep telling her to turn over, to kick somewhere else—oh! There she goes."

Matt met her gaze. His dark eyes were soft and sparkly at the same time. "Wow," he whispered.

She nodded. "I know. Wow."

Matt studied her face for a long moment, his hand never leaving her side, then he bent his head toward hers.

Faith's heartbeat sped up and, reacting to her, the baby's movements became more restless. She chuckled.

"Do you think she'd mind if—"

Faith couldn't stop smiling. "Rub her. She likes to be rubbed."

Matt's strong fingers moved gently against her side, but she couldn't by any definition call what he was doing rubbing. It was more of a soft caress. Nevertheless, the baby settled down.

"She's stopped moving," he whispered.

Faith nodded. "She's gone back to sleep."

"What would happen if—" He stopped, his dark gaze searching hers.

"If?" she whispered.

Matt lowered his head and kissed her. More conflicting sensations slid through her. His lips were soft, yet firm. His kiss was tentative but certainly not shy. And he was disturbingly sexy while at the same time achingly gentle.

Slowly he changed the kiss. He deepened it until Faith thought her legs would give way beneath her. She caught onto his forearms to steady herself as his tongue explored her mouth and played with hers. He tasted like mint toothpaste and sleep.

He pulled her closer, then stopped and looked down. Her belly was pressed against him. She felt his rapid breathing. Matt looked down and back up, and all the tenderness, all the sexiness was gone and in its place was a look of fear.

He stepped backward. "I need to check with Sheriff Hale. Find out if he was able to chase down whoever tossed that brick."

"The brick," Faith repeated, belatedly remembering the note attached to it. "What did the note say?"

Matt looked at her in faint surprise. "I haven't checked it yet." He blinked, then let go of her and looked around until he spotted it where he'd placed it on her dresser, half covered with her robe.

"Have you got gloves?" he asked.

Faith nodded. "Downstairs."

"Good. Let's go get them." Matt picked up the brick, still wrapped in the robe, and they headed downstairs to the kitchen.

Faith gave him a pair of vinyl gloves, and he slid

them on before detaching the note from the brick. He carefully unfolded it as Faith stood beside him.

The sheet of paper was wrinkled and ragged from being tied to the brick, but it was still readable. The message was written in a deliberately childlike hand.

WATCH YOURSELF, FAITH. STAY AWAY FROM POLITICS. IT'S NOT YOUR TIME TO DIE.

Chapter Seven

Matt studied the note and then looked up at Faith. Her eyes were glued to the page and she was frowning.

"I don't understand. What are they talking about?" She looked up at him.

Matt shook his head without commenting. He had an idea what the note was about. He'd bet his salary that it was a warning to her about holding the town hall meeting in her café. He didn't say anything though, because he didn't want to influence Faith before she talked to the sheriff.

At that instant, someone knocked on the door. Faith started. Matt could barely make out the even features of Sheriff Hale through the glass. He'd been expecting him, but he still breathed a sigh of relief as he went to the door and unlocked it.

"Sheriff, hi," Matt said.

"Soarez. Ms. Scott." Hale tipped his cowboy hat, then turned back to Matt. "I drove around for about twenty minutes, looking for the vehicle you saw. Never did see one like you described."

"Thanks for trying," Matt said.

"So where's the brick?"

Matt led the sheriff to the counter where the note was laid out.

The sheriff pulled out his reading glasses and read it quickly, then bent over it and studied it more closely. He grabbed a napkin from a stack sitting on the counter and used it to pick up the paper and turn it over. He held it up to the light for a second, then laid it down again.

"Black ballpoint pen on plain cheap paper, like copy paper. No watermark." He took off his reading glasses and looked at Faith. "You got any idea what this means? *Stay away from politics?*"

Matt waited to see what Faith said. "I—I don't know," she said, spreading her hands miserably. She looked at Matt, but he just stared at her steadily. It wasn't his place to answer for her. He wasn't in the bedroom when the brick came through the window. She needed to give Sheriff Hale her own description of what happened. It wasn't easy to stop himself from going to her and putting his arm around her for reassurance, but he couldn't. He was getting way too caught up in Faith Scott. She wasn't his mission. He was here to make sure no threat got close to Governor Lockhart and no harm came to the townspeople.

He waited to see how she was going to answer the sheriff.

"Maybe it's about the governor? What if someone's upset that I'm hosting the town hall meeting?"

Hale narrowed his eyes. "Are you asking me or telling me?"

Faith started, and her face turned white. Matt doubted the sheriff had ever snapped at her before.

"Why don't you tell me exactly what happened?" Hale went on.

Faith looked at Matt and back at the sheriff. "I really don't know. There was a huge crash, and something landed on the bed. It woke me up." She looked at Matt again, but he didn't speak. "I—I screamed, and then Matt ran in."

"What window did they throw the brick through?"

"My—my bedroom window. It's right over the bed."

"When I ran in and turned on the light, the brick and a huge shard of glass were just about in the middle of the bed."

"And you were here? Sleeping down here?"

"Tonight I was sleeping upstairs." Matt held up a hand. "On the couch. So I was right there as soon as it happened."

The sheriff held Matt's gaze for a second, then turned to Faith again. "Ms. Scott, would you excuse Soarez and me? I just want to go over the technical details with him about the vehicle he saw."

Faith looked a little suspicious, but she agreed. "I'm pretty tired, and Li'l Bit is fussy." She rubbed her side and winced. "I'm going to try to get some sleep." She turned toward the stairs, then stopped. "Oh, no."

Matt knew immediately what the problem was. "You take the couch. It's already made up. Don't touch the bed. Just close the bedroom door. We may need to get more photos. I'll sleep down here."

It looked for a moment like she was going to object, but then she nodded and headed upstairs.

Once Matt heard the door at the top of the stairs close, he turned to Sheriff Hale.

"Well, what do you think?"

Matt shook his head. "I don't know. I'd have to

assume someone is warning her about associating with the governor."

Hale nodded toward the stairs. "Yeah, it does. But if Stockett's still in town, he won't have missed that you're sleeping here."

Matt nodded, leaning against the counter. "That's true. He sure wasn't happy that I stepped in the other night. But throwing a brick through her window? And that cryptic note? I'd expect something more direct from Stockett. Like 'you're mine.'"

"You've got a point. Is Faith afraid of him?"

"Not really. Not physically. She handled him pretty well. She slammed the cash register drawer on his hand."

Hale chuckled. "You didn't tell me that. Good for her."

"What do you know about Stockett?" Matt asked. "Other than he broke Faith's heart and ran off and left her pregnant."

"Word is he got her to loan him a sizable amount of money."

Matt nodded. "She took out a five thousand dollar loan against the café."

Sheriff Hale shook his head in disgust. "I never liked that SOB."

"Even worse, he arranged the loan and got her involved with loan sharks. She now owes ten grand. The muscle came to see her last night."

Hale frowned. "Did he hurt her?"

"Nope. Actually gave her until Sunday. Not that it makes a difference. No money today is the same as no money Sunday."

"It doesn't make sense that the loan shark would use

a brick through the window to send a message they already gave her in person." He ran a hand over his close-cropped hair. "I'm inclined to think you're right. Someone's not happy that she's hosting the town hall meeting."

"Right, and as far as my job's concerned, this is another threat against the governor."

"Well," Sheriff Hale said, "I need to take photos of the scene and get the crime lab in Amarillo to examine that note."

"Yeah. Because regardless of who threw the brick, they came way too close. If that shard of glass had landed an inch or two one way or another, Faith could have been hurt badly or killed."

By THE TIME MATT FINISHED helping Sheriff Hale get photos of the crime scene and bag Faith's bedclothes, shards of glass and all, it was 9:00 a.m. As soon as he made sure that Faith was all right, he headed out to Bellows's estate.

Bellows had just come back from physical therapy, so he was tired and out of sorts. He ran a towel across his face, then nodded to the physical therapist. "That'll be all, thanks." He looked at Matt. "What is it Soarez? Important, I hope. I've got a lot to do to get ready for tomorrow."

"Yes, sir," Matt said. "I need an advance against my salary."

Bellows's blue eyes widened. "An advance," he repeated. "What kind of advance?"

Matt swallowed. He'd known this was going to be hard, even if Bellows was in a good mood. He wasn't, and he looked like he was ready to take it out on Matt.

"Ten thousand, sir." He fully expected Bellows to blow up, but all he did was narrow his gaze.

"Ten thousand. I suppose you have a good reason?"

"With all due respect, that's personal, sir."

Bellows's brows raised. "You might want to rethink that answer, son, if you expect to get that kind of money from me!"

Matt winced. That was what he was afraid of. Bellows was definitely king of his domain. He'd given Matt a well-paying job because Matt had a set of skills Bellows needed. He was a philanthropist, to a point. And Matt knew he was pushing past that point.

"Sir, the Talk of the Town Café's owner, Faith Scott, needs it."

"For what? I don't know Faith, but I knew her grandmother. Eliza left that place to her granddaughter, free and clear. What has she done to get herself into debt like that? And why do you care? More importantly, why should I care?"

Before Matt could answer, Bellows spoke again. "And for God's sake, sit down. You're making me a nervous wreck pacing like that."

Matt hadn't realized he'd been walking back and forth. He must be more nervous than he realized. He sat in the straight-backed chair. "Do you remember me mentioning Rory Stockett, sir?"

"Stockett? Right, Stockett. I asked around. He's generally thought of as a pretty slimy character."

Matt nodded. "He convinced Faith to take out a loan for five thousand dollars."

"So the girl hasn't got any better sense than to trust a snake? That's her problem, isn't it?" Bellows eyed

Matt narrowly. "Come on, Sergeant. You're not getting tangled up with her, are you? Isn't she pregnant?"

"Yes, sir, she is, and no, sir. I'm not."

Matt endured Bart Bellows's intense scrutiny. "Stockett gave her a ring—a fake—and told her as soon as he could get his trucking business started they'd get married. That's what he wanted the money for—supposedly."

Bellows sat back in his wheelchair. "I did some looking into Rory Stockett, using a few connections I've got in various lines of work," he said, an ironic tone creeping into his voice.

Matt could imagine that Bellows's influence extended from the highest government contacts to the lowest fringes of the criminal community.

"He's well-known for his shady dealings and general sliminess." Bellows paused for a second to take a deep breath.

"It's pretty certain that he works for a major loan shark, although knowing the gentleman, I'm surprised he'd put up with Stockett. He also gambles, and he seems to specialize in separating gullible females from their money. I suppose he got Eliza's granddaughter mixed up with loan sharks?"

"Last night a man came to see her. Let's just say he wasn't an accountant. He told her if she didn't pay up her café would burn down. And then early this morning a brick was thrown through her window, burying a six-inch shard of glass in the mattress not four inches from her thigh."

Bellows rolled his wheelchair behind his desk. "She's all right?"

"Yes, sir. No thanks to whoever threw that brick. There was a note attached to it. The note said, 'Watch yourself, Faith. Stay away from politics. It's not your time to die.' And the word *politics* was underlined twice."

"Hmm. That's pretty close to the wording on the note the governor received," Bellows said, rubbing his beard. "It's obviously another threat. You understand that my priority is the governor's safety, don't you? And therefore *your* priority is also the governor's safety?"

"I do, sir. Without question."

"What did Bernie say about it?" Bellows asked.

"He thinks the same thing I do. Whoever threw that brick was warning Faith not to hold the town hall meeting there."

Bellows pulled a folder from a desk drawer and opened it. He flipped through the few sheets of paper in it. Matt was certain it was his records. He was also certain that Bellows didn't really need to look at the pages to remind himself of what was on them. Bellows closed the folder and checked his watch.

"I have an appointment in a few minutes. Here's what I can do. I'll give you ten grand for your girlfriend, but it'll come out of your sisters' scholarship fund."

Matt was surprised and dismayed. He'd been so grateful to Bellows for providing his twin baby sisters the opportunity to go to college. He'd known he'd never be able to pay those fees himself. Now he was sacrificing a sizable chunk of their college money to help a young woman whom he didn't really know. It sounded pretty dumb laid out like that.

"Well, son?"

Matt swallowed. "Sir, my family means everything to me. I've made that clear. But Faith Scott is in danger, and I can't turn my back on her. If it is the loan sharks that are threatening her, then ten thousand dollars is not too much to pay to keep her and her baby safe. I'll get the money for my sisters some other way. I can save it or work a second job."

Bellows had already turned and unlocked a small safe in the wall behind him. He counted out one hundred hundreds and laid the stack on his desk within Matt's reach.

"Sir? I need one more thing."

Bellows's jaw flexed, and he tapped a finger.

Matt felt sweat begin to prick the back of his neck. "I got the license on the vehicle the man was driving. I need it run so I can contact him to pay him the ten thousand."

Shaking his head, Bellows took a silver pen from a silver holder and wrote something on a pad. Then he tore off the sheet and laid it on top of the stack of bills. "Call that number. You'll find the man you're looking for."

Matt picked up the bills and stared at the telephone number written on the scrap of paper. "Yes, sir," he said. "Thank you, sir." He turned to leave.

"Watch out, son," Bellows called after him. "You're going to get your heart stomped on."

Matt turned. "Pardon?"

Bellows picked up the phone. "You heard me. Now I'm late for my appointment."

Matt turned and left. As he walked out to his pickup truck he muttered, "My heart is not involved." But even to himself, it sounded as if he were protesting too much.

FAITH FOLDED THE LAST NAPKIN around the silverware and secured it. She looked at the clock over the door.

She had about a half hour until dinner started—not even enough time to shower and change.

She leaned her elbows on the table and put her head, which was pounding, in her hands. She dreaded tomorrow with a passion. Even Tanya Gossett's assurance that the governor's staff would compensate her for her lost revenue wasn't enough.

Glo came in through the kitchen and reached under the counter for her apron. She shook it out, then tied it around her waist and ran her hands down its front, ironing out the fold lines.

Then she scrutinized Faith with a critical eye.

"Honey, stop worrying about the town hall meeting. The governor's got dozens of people on her staff that do this kind of thing all the time. You're not going to have to worry about it."

"I know they'll take care of what the governor wants. I'm just wondering if I'll still have a café after it's all over."

"Oh, sure you will. I remember the last time Lila did this, years ago. She paid your Gram way more than she expected. That was when she had the booth seats recovered."

Faith sighed. "Probably because they got torn up during the meeting."

"No—well, maybe a couple of 'em got ripped. But she said for ages afterward that it was worth it."

"Well, I hope this is."

The bell over the door sounded. Faith looked up. An old-time cowboy walked in, with pressed jeans and polished boots and a big smile on his face.

She did a double take. It was Henry Kemp. Stealing a glance at Glo, she saw that the older woman's mouth was open. Faith wondered if she looked as shocked as Glo did to see Henry smiling. He *never* smiled.

"Henry," she started, but her voice was croaky with surprise. She cleared her throat and tried again. "Henry, hi."

"Faith, my girl. I just stopped by to make sure everything is ready for Lyric and Lacy's birthday party tomorrow."

Faith felt the blood drain from her face, leaving her light-headed. "Oh. I'm afraid there's going to be a problem with tomorrow."

Henry's big smile disappeared, and in its place was a suspicious glare. "Oh, yeah? And what would that be?"

Faith's throat went dry. Was he baiting her? Surely he'd heard about the town hall meeting. Everyone in town knew about it.

"It's...it's Governor Lockhart's town hall meeting. The café will be closed all day until time for the meeting."

Henry's florid face grew purple with rage. *"Governor Lockhart,"* he said in a mocking tone. "The governor's meeting is going to deprive my little twin great-grandbabies of their birthday surprise. That's just perfect." Henry let loose a few curse words.

"Henry, I am so sorry, but I really didn't have a choice."

"Hell, you think I don't know that? Damn Lila Lockhart gets anything she wants, just like all the Lockharts. If they can't get it by legal means, they'll just up and take it. Just like they took my land and didn't give me not one penny for the oil."

"I'll make it up to you. Why don't you and the girls

come in Monday afternoon. Their banana splits and whatever else you want will be my treat. And you'll have the place to yourselves."

Henry's face lost a bit of its purple stain. "It's not your fault, Faith. And I can pay for my own great-grandaughters' birthday treats." He took a couple of steps backward, toward the door. Then he lifted his arm and wagged his forefinger at her. "But you mark my words. This isn't the end of this. Lila's going to be sorry she ruined my girls' birthday. One way or another, she'll be sorry."

He turned on his boot heel and stomped out the door.

"Sheez," Glo breathed. "He was fighting mad."

Faith shivered. "He gets so angry it worries me. Did you see how dark red his face got? I'm afraid he's going to have what Gram called an apoplexy one day." She took a shaky breath. "What do you think he meant when he said Lila would be sorry?"

Glo met her gaze. "I don't know, but the way he said it spooked me."

"Me, too," Faith agreed.

THAT EVENING MATT WENT to his apartment to shower and change. He took a few minutes to put a coat of varnish on the crib, which needed it after standing up through Matt's infancy and his sisters.

He headed over to the café around eight o'clock. As he drove up, he saw a dark figure slip around the side of the building. It looked like Rory Stockett. The height and weight were about right, and Stockett would know that the door to the kitchen stayed open until nine o'clock.

Matt parked and headed around the building behind the stealthy figure. He didn't even try to stay quiet. Gravel crunched under his boots. In the light from a streetlamp, Matt could see that it was Stockett. Just as the man got to the kitchen door he noticed Matt.

He growled audibly and lunged for the doorknob.

"Hold it right there, Stockett."

"You! Get away from me," Stockett said. He tried to turn the knob, but Matt pushed him away.

Stockett stumbled backward, nearly losing his footing. He took a second or two to right himself. He came at Matt, but Matt was ready for him. The con man fought like a schoolkid on a playground, fists doubled and flailing wildly. Matt had no trouble dodging his blows, but Stockett's fury kept him swinging.

Matt landed a blow to Stockett's stomach. That stopped him. He doubled over with a whoosh of breath and fell back against the brick wall of the café.

"What did I tell you about showing up here again?" Matt said, standing over him.

Stockett was still bent over. He coughed a couple of times, then slowly got his feet under him and prepared to stand. By the time Matt saw the glint of steel, it was almost too late.

Stockett came at him like a bull that's seen red, a knife clutched in his fist and his arm raised above his shoulder.

Matt fell back, balancing on the balls of his feet and preparing to deflect Stockett's attack. The other man wasn't a pro with a knife. The way he held it in his fist told Matt that. He sidestepped Stockett's rush, timing it so he could grab his wrist. He almost missed though, when his bum knee nearly gave way when he stepped sideways.

Recovering quickly, he twisted Stockett's arm behind his back. His thumb searched for the pressure point on the inside of his wrist that would paralyze his fingers and force him to drop the knife.

But by this time Stockett was enraged. He struggled, and the knife blade slid across Matt's forearm. Shock made Matt loosen his grip.

Stockett whipped around, barely missing Matt's chest as he ducked backward and stumbled, thanks to his bum knee. With three seconds, he'd recovered his balance. He whirled, aiming a roundhouse kick at Stockett's extended arm.

He connected. The knife clattered to the ground. Ignoring his cut, Matt elbowed Stockett in the temple, then jerked him up by his collar and slammed him against the brick wall.

"What did I tell you about coming back here?"

"You can't tell me what to do! Faith's mine!" Stockett yelped. "She's my fiancée."

Matt got his bloody forearm under Stockett's chin. "No, she's not," he growled between clenched teeth. "You're just the sperm bank."

Stockett struggled, but all Matt had to do to stop him was push a little harder against his throat.

He gurgled.

"If I catch you around here again, you're going to jail for stalking."

"Don't threaten me, you—"

Matt put more pressure on Stockett's throat. "Now get out of here, and don't bother Faith again."

Stockett tried to speak but couldn't. A part of Matt's

brain registered the sound of the kitchen door opening, letting light pour out into the alley.

"Do you understand?" he asked Stockett.

With difficulty, the other man nodded.

Matt grabbed his collar again and shoved him toward the street.

Once Stockett was out of Matt's reach, he turned back. "I'll get you for this, whoever you are. You are a dead man."

Matt laughed. "The name's Soarez. Matt Soarez."

"Matt!" It was Valerio. "What the hell's going on out here? Should I call the sheriff?"

"No," Matt replied, watching to make sure Stockett was really gone. "It was just that slimebag Stockett. I had to remind him that he's not welcome around here."

"Good for you. Now come inside and have some dinner."

Matt followed Valerio into the kitchen, where Faith was pulling a freshly baked pan of rolls from the oven. "What was going on out there, Valerio?"

She glanced up and almost dropped the pan. "Matt! What happened? You're bleeding."

He'd almost forgotten about the cut on his forearm. He looked down at it. *Damn*. It was deeper than he'd thought. "Valerio," he said. "Would you mind taking a towel and picking up the knife out there? It might come in handy if I decide to charge Stockett with assault."

"Rory?" Faith gasped. "Rory did this?"

"He was sneaking around by your kitchen door. I told him to go away."

"Oh, Matt. We've got to stop that bleeding." She picked up a fresh kitchen towel and wrapped it around his arm. "You're going to need stitches."

"I don't think so—"

"Of course, you are. We need to get you to over to Holy Cross Hospital. It's only five miles away. I'll drive you. Glo can close down tonight. Since we won't be opening at all tomorrow, I can close out the register in the morning."

Matt started to object, but he knew Faith was right. The pressure of the towel against the cut had increased the throbbing to a level that could definitely be called pain, and so far, the bleeding hadn't slowed down. "I can drive myself," he protested.

"No, you can't. Now let's go." Faith's mouth was set, and her eyes sparked with determination. He hadn't known her long, but he knew that look. There was no changing her mind.

Chapter Eight

Dr. Larry Kendall was the doctor on call in the emergency room at Holy Cross Hospital. When he came into the examining room, he greeted Faith warmly.

"How's that ankle?" he asked her as he unwrapped the bloody towel from Matt's arm.

She stuck her foot out. "It's fine," she said. "My ego still aches though."

Dr. Kendall laughed. "In the first month or so of her pregnancy, Faith slipped on a French fry and twisted her ankle. What happened here, Mr.—"

"Soarez. Matt Soarez. I ran into a little trouble in an alley."

Faith jumped in. "He stopped the baby's father from breaking in to the café," she said. "Rory attacked him with a knife."

Dr. Kendall assessed Matt. "You know I'm obligated to report this to the police."

Matt's lips thinned, and he nodded.

Faith rubbed the side of her tummy. She hadn't known that knife wounds had to be reported. Rory might be arrested, and Faith wasn't exactly sure how she felt about that. She knew for a fact that she would never allow Rory in her life again. But he was also the baby's father. It hurt her to think he would have a record.

Dr. Kendall prodded and squeezed Matt's arm. "Well, Faith is right," he said. "You do need stitches."

He grabbed a plastic basin off a shelf and opened a bottle labeled Sterile Saline. He irrigated Matt's arm as he talked. Matt grimaced.

Faith shivered. She was sure that the liquid pouring over the open cut burned.

"So who are you, Mr. Soarez? I don't believe I've ever seen you around this area."

"That's right. I'm in town temporarily, working on a construction project."

"And you just happened to be at Faith's café tonight when her ex showed up?"

"He—Matt's been doing some work for me," Faith said quickly.

"I see," Kendall said. He pulled a bottle labeled Povidone-Iodine down from the shelf and irrigated the wound with the brown, strong-smelling liquid. Matt sat stoically, but his face paled.

The doctor was nodding. "I think you're going to need at least five—maybe six. We'll see how it goes."

"I've got to be able to work tomorrow."

Dr. Kendall looked up at Matt from over the rims of his glasses. "Well, we'll see about that."

It didn't take the doctor a minute to neatly tie off six sutures in Matt's forearm. Finally, he wrapped gauze around the wound and taped it. "There you go. You'll need to get back in here in five days or so and get the stitches taken out." Kendall sent Matt a knowing look. "Meanwhile, take it easy."

"Don't worry, Doctor," Faith said. "I'm going to make sure he doesn't hurt those stitches."

Kendall reached for the button on the intercom. "I need to have the admissions clerk call the police."

"Doctor," Matt said. "Wait a minute."

Kendall turned and gave Matt a suspicious look.

"I'd like a couple of minutes to talk with you before you make that report."

Kendall's eyes narrowed. "Go ahead."

Matt sent Faith a glance. "In private."

The doctor assessed him. "Give me a minute, then," he said and turned to Faith. "Are you seeing your ob/gyn regularly?"

She nodded. "Sure. In fact, I have an appointment next week."

He pointed at her feet. "Mind if I have a look?" He didn't wait for an answer. He sat and gently tugged her pant leg up, first right and then left. "Hmm."

He leaned down to press gently on the skin around her ankles. "How has your blood pressure been?"

"Dr. Jones said it was a little high."

The doctor nodded. "I don't suppose you remember the numbers? See how swollen your feet are? Is this happening a lot?"

"Well, not a lot. Dr. Jones mentioned it last week. He told me to stay off my feet as much as possible."

Dr. Kendall looked up at her. "And have you?"

Faith nodded. "It's just been busy, you know."

The look Dr. Kendall gave her was filled with censure and concern. "Has Dr. Jones talked to you about pre-eclampsia?" He asked as he took her blood pressure.

Faith nodded. She hadn't understood a lot of what her ob/gyn had said. He talked fast and used a lot of medical terminology. But she did understand that it was dangerous.

"Have you been having headaches? Nausea? Vomiting?"

Faith had to admit that she had been experiencing all those symptoms. "But like I said—"

"You've been busy. I know. Well, your pressure is definitely high. It's not dangerously high, which is good, or I'd have to admit you. And while your ankles are swollen, they're not too bad. If any of your symptoms worsen, I will put you into the hospital. Understand?"

Faith nodded miserably. "I understand, but I can't go into the—"

"Listen to me, Faith. I'm *ordering* you to stay off your feet unless it's absolutely necessary." He shook his finger at her. "I'm talking no more than a couple of hours a day. *And* I'm ordering you to call Dr. Jones tomorrow—well, make that Monday, since tomorrow's Saturday."

Dr. Kendall turned and looked at Matt, who nodded resolutely. Faith had no doubt that he would make sure Dr. Kendall's orders were followed to the letter.

"And," he said again, "if anything happens over the weekend, I'm on call here." He turned to Matt again. "I'm assuming you two are close? You bring her in."

"Close?" Faith said, her voice tinged with panic that even she could hear. "No. Well, I mean—"

"Bring her in," Dr. Kendall repeated.

Dr. Kendall picked up the folder that sat on the gurney beside Matt and made some notes. Then he pulled a blank form out of a drawer and wrote some more. He handed the single form to Faith.

"Give this to the admissions clerk, and don't forget

what I said. Come to the E.R. here if anything happens over the weekend, and call Dr. Jones on Monday."

Faith nodded. She looked at Matt, who sent her a small smile. "I'll just wait out here, then."

Matt nodded.

As soon as Dr. Kendall closed the door behind Faith, Matt spoke. "I have a couple of requests, Doctor."

"Okay." Dr. Kendall set the folder down and crossed his arms.

"When I said I have to be able to work tomorrow, I meant it. I specialize in surveillance," he said.

Dr. Kendall picked up the folder again. "You listed your job as construction worker."

"That's right. My cover is as a construction worker doing a job for Bart Bellows."

Dr. Kendall's eyebrows shot up.

"In fact, my assignment for tomorrow could be a matter of national security."

"National—?" Dr. Kendall laughed.

Matt pulled a card out of his wallet and showed it to the doctor. "This is Bart Bellows's personal card. You're welcome to call his home number and verify this."

Dr. Kendall read the card, then raised his gaze to Matt's. "Why don't you tell me what your job is tomorrow."

Matt wondered how much he should reveal to the doctor. "You said you're on duty here in the E.R. this weekend? And this is the closest emergency room to Freedom?"

Dr. Kendall nodded to both questions.

"That's good. There's a definite possibility that we could have injuries. Let me go over what's happening tomorrow." Matt quickly explained about the threats against Governor Lockhart and the town hall meeting the governor was holding at the Talk of the Town Café.

"There are a number of trained experts, including myself, the governor's bodyguards and police from Amarillo, who will be on hand to help Sheriff Hale maintain order," he finished.

Dr. Kendall shook his head and uttered a short laugh. "Well, I do believe this is the first time I've had the opportunity to treat an undercover agent."

"Now for the other request," Matt said.

"All right." Dr. Kendall pushed his glasses up on his nose and waited.

"I'd like to ask that you not report this incident to the authorities."

Kendall looked dubious but not as determined as he had before. "We're required to by law," he said.

"Then could you delay your report for a few days? The man who attacked me is Rory Stockett. He's the father of Faith's baby, but he's also a person of interest in a couple of matters. While it would make me feel a whole hell of a lot better if he were behind bars, putting him in jail might spook the people we're trying to catch."

"Sounds to me like locking him up would make Governor Lockhart a lot safer."

Matt nodded. "For tomorrow. But these threats have been escalating. And I can guarantee you that Stockett is small potatoes. We're targeting the mastermind. Only when we can stop whoever's behind the threats will Governor Lockhart be safe. And not before."

ON THE DRIVE BACK to the café, Faith glanced over at Matt, who was staring at the bandage on his forearm. "What was that all about?" she asked.

"What?" he seemed to have trouble tearing his eyes away from his injured arm.

"You and Dr. Kendall. You know I'm doing fine taking care of myself."

Matt's jaw clenched. Faith could see the lights from oncoming cars playing off the clean planes of his cheek and jaw. She parked in the lot behind the café.

"There's such a thing as doctor–patient privilege," she said archly, even though she knew that whatever Matt had wanted to talk to Dr. Kendall about in private had little if anything to do with her. There was something else going on.

The moment Matt had walked in, his arm slashed and bleeding, she'd confirmed her suspicion that he was more than a drifter. Gone was the small smile, the shy ducking of his head, his graceful, lanky ease of movement.

The man who stalked into the kitchen and ordered Valerio to pick up the knife as evidence, who'd shown an odd lack of concern over a wound that ended up taking six stitches, was no simple itinerant worker.

No. Matteo Soarez was more than he seemed, more than he wanted her to know.

"It wasn't about you," he said flatly.

"I know that," she snapped.

"Dr. Kendall said he'd be on duty in the E.R. tomorrow. I wanted to give him a heads-up about the governor's town hall meeting in case anyone gets hurt."

"You don't think the governor's staff might have already taken care of that?" She unfastened her seat belt.

"Wait," Matt said, laying a hand on her arm.

Faith stopped and turned toward him. "What is it?"

"You're right. The governor's staff has definitely covered everything. The reason I spoke to Dr. Kendall is because I've been asked to help with security for the town hall meeting. Among other things, I'll be keeping an eye on the crowd while Governor Lockhart is speaking."

Matt's tone hadn't changed. Faith searched his face. Was he lying? It didn't sound like a lie exactly, but it didn't sound like the truth either.

She was exhausted. Her feet hurt, as did her head. The baby was kicking her in the side, and Dr. Kendall's warning about preeclampsia had frightened her. So she wasn't in the mood to play verbal ping-pong.

"Why you?" she bit out, hearing the faint derision that colored her words.

Matt's head jerked slightly, hardly enough to notice, but she saw it and felt it.

"Why me?" he repeated on a short laugh. "The obvious. Extra muscle. And I can use the money."

Faith immediately regretted her attitude. "I didn't mean—"

Matt held up a hand. "I know. No problem."

"No, you don't know. I'm too suspicious of—people." She'd started to say *men*. "I tend to start out thinking the worst these days."

Matt's dark eyes went soft, and his mouth relaxed into a brief smile. "I'm not Stockett," he murmured.

She couldn't hold his gaze. There was a question in it, a question Faith wasn't sure she could answer. She'd worked hard to build a life for herself and the baby she was carrying. After eight long months, she'd finally convinced herself that she could do it alone. She had the café. She had Glo, who was almost like a mother to her. She had her friends.

What use did she have for another man who, as she'd told Glo, didn't have two dimes to rub together?

Matt touched her cheek with his thumb. "I understand how much he hurt you. And I know how hard it is to face becoming a mother when you're alone. I watched my mother struggle to keep our family together after my dad left."

Faith lifted her gaze to his. "I don't want—" Matt's forefinger pressed against her lips before she could say "another drifter in my life."

Before she could react, he leaned forward and pressed a gentle kiss on her mouth.

To her dismay, she moaned at the feel of his mouth on hers. It was a moan of frustration, of need. Her body remembered their previous kiss and all the sensations he'd evoked in her.

Matt pulled away, his eyes locked with hers and the question in them was unmistakable.

Then she did something else she couldn't believe she was doing. She leaned toward him. She kissed him, and it was no gentle kiss either.

He gasped, then kissed her back. His mouth was firm and not quite so gentle this time.

Unlike Rory, whose kisses had been hot and exciting and nearly frantic, Matt's were deep and slow and infinitely more arousing.

They felt like they came from his soul and touched hers. She felt cherished, cared-for, safe. Yet at the same time, her body flowed with desire that surpassed anything she'd ever experienced.

"Matt?" Faith whispered against his mouth. "If—"

For a couple of seconds, Matt continued kissing her, his hand cradling her head. Then he stopped and pulled away. His cheeks were flushed. He gave her a tender look. "Hmm?"

Faith felt heat rush to her face, to match the heat inside her. "I said if you want we could—"

He shook his head. "No," he said harshly. Then his thumb slid caressingly across the line of her jaw. His face softened. "No," he repeated gently. "Faith, I hope you can understand what I'm about to say. Maybe you won't right now, but I hope you will soon."

A frisson of fear and dread slid up her spine. She recognized the tone. She'd heard it before. It was the brush-off.

"I'm not about stealing a few kisses here and there, or quickie hookups that last only as long as I'm in town."

She shook her head. "So what's the deal? You have a girlfriend? That's okay." She reached for the driver side door handle and opened the door.

"Faith." He grasped her by the arm. "Look at me."

She turned her gaze to his, hoping the tears she could feel gathering in her throat didn't show in her eyes.

"I don't have a girlfriend," he said, emphasizing each word. "Or a wife."

"Fine," she said flatly. She had no idea if she could trust him. The only thing she knew for certain was that she had lousy judgment when it came to men.

What would she give to just once find that her feelings about someone were correct? To her, Matt seemed like a loyal, caring, honorable man—the kind who falls in love once and commits to that person for the whole of his life.

She turned in the seat to climb awkwardly out of the car, muttering, "Why can't I be right this time?"

"What?" Matt said, opening the passenger side door and rushing around the car to take her hand and help her out. "What did you say?"

"Nothing," she said quickly. "I was...I was talking to the baby."

His keen look told her that he didn't believe that for one second.

Faith, now that she was standing, pulled her hand away from Matt's gentle grip, but he resisted. Instead, he tugged her along with him, up the steps and around to the kitchen door, which he opened with his key.

Then he led her through the kitchen and up the stairs to her apartment.

His hand cradling hers felt strong and protective— and oddly like the end of a date. At the door to her bedroom, he tugged on her hand until she turned to face him. The expression on his face seemed to be pleased and a little bit triumphant.

"Faith," he said, looking down at their hands, "I have something for you, and I don't want you to even think about refusing it."

She couldn't fathom what he was talking about. "Something for me? What?"

"Just a minute." He let go of her hand and went to the sofa that he was using as a bed. He lifted a seat cushion and retrieved a thick manila folder, then came back to stand in front of her.

"This," he said, holding out the folder.

Faith stared at it uncomprehendingly. "I don't understand," she said.

"This is the money to pay back your loan."

"Oh." Shock sent prickles like a thousand needles through her limbs to her fingers and toes. "Oh, no." She held up her hands, palm out. "No, I can't take that. Oh, Matt, where did you get it?"

"Don't worry," he said, still holding it out toward her. "It's an advance on my salary, and unlike Stockett, I have total confidence that you'll pay me back."

"No, Matt." Faith shook her head. She couldn't think straight. Matt, a nearly perfect stranger, was offering her a way out of the looming debt that Rory had gotten her into. He was offering her money to save her café.

Matt put his finger against her lips. "Don't argue with me. You won't win. What time did the man say he'd be back to collect the money?"

Faith pulled away. When Matt touched her mouth she couldn't think. "He didn't say."

"Okay. I've got a number that I can call. I'll keep the cash and make arrangements to meet him. That'll be better anyhow. I don't like the idea of you meeting with him alone."

"But, Matt, I can't pay you back. I don't have that kind of money."

"Don't worry about it. We'll work out a repayment schedule once all this town hall business is finished."

Faith felt tears fill her eyes. "I don't know what to say. I—"

"Shh," he whispered, his finger against her lips again. "You don't have to say a word. Now get some sleep. You've got an incredibly busy day tomorrow." He turned and went to the couch and began spreading out the sheets and plumping the pillow.

Faith went into her bedroom and closed the door. She'd gotten a glimpse inside the envelope when Matt had held it out. What she'd seen had turned her legs to jelly. She'd seen more hundred dollar bills than she'd ever seen in one place in her life.

She looked at the door, feeling Matt's overwhelming presence in the next room. First he appointed himself her protector, then her personal warrior against Rory Stockett's unwanted attention. And now this man who was to all accounts nothing more than an itinerant worker was bailing her out of debt.

As tears streamed down her face, her mind was filled with one question.

Who was Matt Soarez?

Chapter Nine

"So while I *do not* take these threats lightly, they will not sway me from my pledge to the people of the wonderful state of Texas!" At the mention of the state of Texas, the standing-room-only crowd, which filled the Talk of the Town Café and spilled out into the street, burst into cheers and applause.

Cameras flashed and reporters clutching microphones crowded around the lunch counter, which formed a natural barrier to the makeshift stage with workers had built.

Governor Lila Lockhart, radiating energy and confidence from the podium, paused until the noise died down. She glanced at each of the cameras in turn, allotting equal time to each network.

Matt grimaced inwardly. He'd have preferred that she not mention the threats, and he knew Bart Bellows felt the same way. But Bellows had told him the governor was "as stubborn as a mule on a hot August day."

He let his gaze travel over the crowd, not zeroing in on any particular face. Trying to read faces in this crowd that were stuffed into Faith's small diner and spilling out the doors was futile.

Instead, he set his brain to scan for impressions. It

was a tactic he'd perfected overseas—a tactic that had worked almost every time. He thought regretfully of his best friend Rusty, who had died because Matt hadn't believed a mother with a child would plant a lethal bomb.

Tonight he was fighting to keep his attention a hundred percent on his job. A small part of his brain kept turning to Faith.

He was acutely conscious of where she was standing, beside the mayor, near the kitchen door. He'd done his best to get her to stay upstairs in her apartment and avoid the stress and turmoil, but she'd refused.

This was her diner, and she was going to watch over it during the speech, she'd told him.

Governor Lockhart hadn't cornered the market on stubbornness.

"This is why I've come back to Freedom, my hometown," the governor continued, "to renew my promise to you, my friends and neighbors, and to the people of Texas, that I am *still* working for *you*."

"Liar!" Even through the cheers and applause, the single word split the air like a thunderbolt. Next to Matt, one of the governor's bodyguards stiffened and put his hand on the taser attached to his belt.

Cameras swerved in the direction of the outburst, and the mutterings of the crowd buzzed through the café's dining room.

Matt immediately zeroed in on the speaker. It was Henry Kemp. He muttered Kemp's name and location into his com unit and received a response from Farraday, who was standing at the governor's right side.

"At ease," Farraday said as the crowd noise turned to

a cacophony of cheers and jeers. "Just a heckler. She'll handle it."

Lila held up a hand, gesturing for quiet. She laughed easily. "And this," she said, then paused to wait for the crowd to quiet down before she continued, "*this* is what I love about our great country and our great state of Texas! Any citizen has the right to voice his own opinion—even a grouchy old curmudgeon."

Laughter broke the tension in the room. Governor Lockhart had the crowd back—the crowd and the cameras.

Matt turned his attention back to Henry, to see how he'd taken Lila's subtle put-down. As he did, his brain registered something that wasn't right. He'd seen the glint of light on cold steel.

It took only a split second for the message from his brain of what he saw to reach his lips, but by the time it did it was already too late.

"Gun!" he shouted as a second flash drew his eyes and the shot echoed in the confines of the café.

A shriek of pain came from behind him, followed immediately by a shout. "Call an ambulance. We've got one down!"

He didn't have time to even turn his head to see who had been hit. Lockhart's bodyguards were taking care of her. Matt needed to catch the shooter.

Suddenly everything seemed to be moving in slow motion. Every move he made was too slow. He kept his gaze on the area where he'd seen the flash as he leaped over the lunch counter into the crowd.

"Blue baseball cap! Light blue shirt. Mustache! Behind Kemp and to his left!" He recited the description of the man he'd seen holding the gun into his com unit. "Heading for the front doors. Stop him! Don't let him get away!"

For a couple of seconds, he felt as if he were body-surfing as he was propelled along on the shoulders of the panicked crowd. Finally he got his feet on the floor and started moving in the direction he'd seen the baseball cap move. But the cap was nowhere to be seen. What a ridiculously simple disguise. They should have disallowed any headgear inside the café. But it was too late now.

Behind him he heard shouts and a scuffle as the governor's bodyguards whisked her away through the kitchen. Go with them, he silently ordered Faith.

He pushed his way past the screaming, frightened crowd, a slow process—too slow. He should have gone out through the kitchen and around. *Damn it.*

"Hale, I've lost him," he said, but his com unit was buzzing with chatter. Farraday shouted orders. One of the bodyguards was groaning in pain. Deputy Sheriff Appleton was trying to calm the crowd.

"Sheriff! Do you have him?" he shouted.

Finally he was able to pick Sheriff Hale's even-toned voice out of the chatter. "Negative. No sign of him."

A hand grabbed his arm. Matt whirled, his fists doubled, ready to fight. It was a reporter. A foam-covered microphone was thrust in his face.

"You were on the platform with the governor. What can you tell us?"

"Get the hell out of my way," he growled. He pushed the microphone away and forced his way through the crowd to the door. He saw the sheriff headed his way. Matt turned the volume down on his com unit. The sheriff caught his eye and did the same.

"Crowd's too big and too out of control. No sense in trying to hold 'em," Hale said.

Matt wanted to protest. His first instinct was to round up the entire crowd and test them all for gunshot residue on their hands, but he knew the sheriff was right. Whoever had taken the shot had long since disappeared into the melee and by now could be as far as the edge of town.

"Damned easy disguise," Hale muttered.

"Tell me about it. All he had to do was take off the cap. He was tall though."

Sheriff Hale nodded and rubbed a hand over his head. "Not tall enough."

Matt snorted. "Yeah." From what he'd seen, the shooter was probably about six feet tall—taller than many of the people in the café but certainly not tall enough to stand out without that blue cap on.

Another reporter was headed their way. Matt turned his back on her and caught the sheriff's eye. He gestured with his head.

The sheriff put a finger to the earpiece of his com unit, listening. "Okay," he said. "Get the officers back here, and let's get this crowd dispersed."

Matt turned up the volume on his unit. Deputy Appleton was talking. Behind him, Matt could hear Farraday speaking through his com unit.

"No one with a baseball cap seen leaving past the perimeter."

"One bodyguard shot. Shoulder wound."

"Mayor Arkwright and Ms. Scott were knocked down. Both seem to be fine."

Faith! Matt's heart skipped. She'd been standing right by the kitchen door. The bodyguards, in their dash to get Governor Lockhart to safety, had rushed the doors to the kitchen and trampled the mayor and Faith.

Dear God, he hoped she hadn't been hurt.

Torn between his duty and his worry for Faith, Matt looked at the sheriff, who nodded.

"Go ahead," Hale said. "I've got this."

FAITH FROWNED AT MATT and pushed his hand away from her forehead again. "I told you, I'm fine," she said irritably. The flashing red lights of the ambulance were turning her headache into a migraine, she was feeling queasy and her elbow throbbed where she'd scraped it on the door hinge.

"According to the EMT, your blood pressure's up. And Dr. Kendall said he'd put you in the hospital if—"

"If it went too high," she finished. "It's not. Now please, stop fussing. *This* is a scraped elbow," she continued, pointing at the burning scratches. "*That* is a gunshot wound," she gestured toward the EMTs, who were loading the wounded bodyguard into the ambulance, hindered in their efforts by the gaggle of reporters and cameramen crowded around the ambulance doors.

Matt sent her an exasperated look. "The bodyguard's got a flesh wound in his shoulder. And *he's* not pregnant."

"Ha ha," she retorted. "Now if you'll get out of my way, I need to take a look at the damage to my café." She moved to rise, but her shaky legs didn't seem to want to work. She didn't want to tell Matt, but for a few seconds after the gunshot rang out, she'd been afraid she and the baby would be trampled.

The governor's bodyguards had wasted no time in grabbing Lila Lockhart and the injured guard and boldy carrying them off the stage and through the kitchen, without regard to anyone standing in their path.

The mayor had been shoved into the counter and had the breath knocked out of him. Faith was thankful she'd been behind him or it would have been her tummy—her baby—slamming into the sharp wooden edge of the counter.

As it was, she'd been knocked aside by a guard. She'd fallen against the kitchen door's frame and scraped her elbow on the hinge. The only thing that had kept her from tumbling to the ground and being trampled was that her blouse had caught on the hinge.

"Damn it, Faith," Matt snapped. "If you'd just done what Dr. Kendall said, you'd have been upstairs out of harm's way."

He put a hand out to steady her as she stood. "Now look at you. You can't even walk by yourself. Didn't the governor's staff tell you they'd take care of the damage? Come on. I'm taking you upstairs and putting you to bed, where you should have been all along."

She opened her mouth.

"Or I can call Dr. Kendall, and you know what he'll do," he said sternly.

Faith didn't protest again. It had been a long, exhausting day. As Matt's strong arm around her waist helped her up the stairs, she asked, "What about the shooter? Did they catch him?"

"Nope. He was wearing a baseball cap, so all he had to do was drop the cap and he'd be indistinguishable from the rest of the crowd."

"He was trying to kill Governor Lockhart?" she asked as Matt guided her through the crowd, into the café and up the stairs.

He nodded grimly as he unlocked her door. "He was standing behind Henry Kemp."

Faith stepped inside her living room and sat heavily on the couch. "Oh. I forgot to tell you. Henry came into the café yesterday afternoon. He wanted to check on the plans for his great-grandaughters' birthday treat. He'd told me last week he wanted to bring them in this afternoon for banana splits. But I had to tell him he couldn't do it today because of the town hall meeting."

Matt nodded. "I'll bet he was real happy about that," he said sarcastically.

"Matt, he...he *threatened* her. I mean, sort of. He said she'd be sorry she spoiled his great-grandaughters' party—'one way or another,' he said."

Matt's mouth went grim. "I'm afraid he's gone round the bend about this feud with the Lockharts. Look how he yelled out that she was a liar in front of all those people and the TV cameras!"

"I know. I was surprised that he did that. It's really not like him."

Matt's brow furrowed. "Not like him? He blasts the governor every chance he gets. Look at what you just told me he did yesterday."

"I know. It worried me. His face turned purple. I was afraid he'd have a heart attack. But I don't think he'd actually do anything. He's a big blowhard, and he'll never get over what he thinks the Lockharts did to his family, but he's got a granddaughter and beautiful twin great-granddaughters. He'd rather take a bullet himself than do anything to hurt them."

Matt looked at her sharply. "That's exactly what I told—" He stopped and dropped his gaze.

"Told who?"

He clenched his jaw. He had to be more careful. He'd almost blown his cover by mentioning that he'd talked with Bart Bellows about Kemp.

"Matt?"

He looked back at her. "Never mind. Are you okay?" he asked, then smiled. "Want me to help you get ready for bed?"

There was nothing Faith would like better than to have Matt stay with her. Her tummy hurt where the baby was pressing against her right side, and her headache was making her feel nauseated. It throbbed painfully with every heartbeat. She squeezed her eyes closed for a second.

"Faith? Are you hurting?"

She shook her head. "No, I'm fine." She shooed him with her hands. "Go on and do your body guarding thing. I'm going to sleep."

He searched her face, then nodded. "I'll be up in a little while. I'll look in on you."

Matt left, and she heard his footsteps going down the stairs. It didn't take her but a couple of minutes to wash and bandage her elbow. She changed into her nightgown and crawled under the covers.

She leaned back against the pillows and tried to relax. When she did, she felt the familiar ache in her tummy. She rubbed it. "Settle down, Li'l Bit," she whispered. "Mommy's head is hurting really badly. We need to go to sleep, okay?"

But she didn't feel sleepy. She felt anxious. The throbbing in her head seemed to be spreading through her whole body. She could feel her pulse in her fingers and toes.

She wished Matt were here. It was so much easier to

fall asleep when she knew he was on the couch in the living room.

Matt's protective care and his concern about her were addicting. She loved that he worried about her, that he was determined to keep her safe. She loved that he teased her.

She loved everything about him, she thought sleepily. He was downstairs, and when he finished, he'd come up to her apartment and place himself between her and the door. Between her and danger.

How was she going to live without him once he was gone?

MATT FOUND SHERIFF HALE studying the floor of the café as if the debris left there by the crowd would yield up its secrets if he stared long enough.

"Sheriff?"

Hale didn't look up. "I was hoping to find a clue." He chuckled wryly. "Hell, I was hoping to walk in here and see a baseball cap lying in the middle of the floor." He glanced up at Matt. "That'd make our lives a lot easier."

"I can't argue with that," Matt responded. "Any other news?"

Hale ran a hand over his close-cropped hair. "The bodyguard's wound was a through-and-through. We haven't found the bullet yet."

He nodded toward the lunch counter, behind which was the temporary stage the governor's staff had built for the town hall meeting. "I'm betting it fell under the stage. The workers will be in tomorrow morning to dismantle it. I'm going to be right there. Maybe that bullet will give us a lead."

Matt hoped so. "What else?"

"Not much else we can do. Fingerprints are out, considering the size of the crowd and what I know about Freedom. I'd guesstimate that less than half the population has ever been printed."

"And of course nobody saw anything."

"Not a thing. Moncel Jefferson, a senior in high school, was standing right in the doorway. He tells me that after the shot rang out a guy nearly ran him over getting out the door. Moncel says he grabbed the guy's arm and asked him if he saw anything, but the guy jerked away and nearly knocked Moncel down."

"Can Moncel describe him?" Matt asked hopefully, but the sheriff was already shaking his head.

"He said the man had on a long-sleeved shirt with the sleeves rolled up. Said he thought it was blue. And jeans. That's all."

"That fits with what I remember. Did he mention the baseball cap?"

Hale sighed. "According to Moncel, he wasn't wearing one, but he can't remember the guy's face. Said he was a white guy. Average looking. Tall."

"Not much to go on," Matt said.

"Nope," the sheriff agreed.

Chapter Ten

Faith had a huge blood pressure cuff wrapped around her middle and the doctor was tightening it—tighter, tighter until she couldn't breathe.

"Faith!"

She woke with a start. "Matt?" she gasped. She looked down at herself. There was nothing wrapped around her, yet she still felt the squeezing pain.

He took her hand and sat on the edge of her bed. "You were dreaming," he said with a small smile.

Faith closed her eyes and moaned. She was used to her tummy hurting, but this was different. Her lower abdomen, her back, even her thighs hurt. She pushed up to a sitting position and moaned again.

Matt frowned at her. "What's the matter?"

"Nothing," she answered irritably. "It just a pain. It'll go away—" She gasped as the pain intensified. Now it felt more like a cramp.

"Come on. You're in labor. We need to get you to the hospital."

"No. I told you—" Faith said between clenched teeth "—it will go away." And it did. She collapsed back against the pillows and sighed. "See?"

But Matt didn't look relieved. "How long has this been going on?" he asked.

"It hasn't. I was dreaming." But as she said the words, she realized the squeezing, cramping pain had happened before—a couple of times. She'd woken up, barely, then gone back to sleep.

"How far apart?"

"Stop it," she said. "I'm not in labor," she paused, embarrassed, but decided that she'd rather be a little bit embarrassed than be hauled off to the hospital for a false alarm. "My water hasn't even broken yet."

Matt didn't bat an eye. He was obviously unimpressed by her statement. He looked at his watch. "Get dressed. I'm going downstairs to let Valerio know we're going to the hospital." He turned toward the door.

"Matt, don't get him and Glo all worked up. These are not contractions."

He turned back, and his dark eyes sparked with determination. "Get dressed, or I'll carry you downstairs like that. I'll be back in a couple of minutes."

Faith stared at the back of his head until he disappeared through the door. She'd never been looked at like that, never been spoken to like that. She lay there for a moment, trying to decipher the look on his face and in his eyes.

There was determination and authority. but there was something else, too. It was something fierce and protective—almost primal.

If she weren't huge and round and exhausted, she could believe Matt cared about her. But in the first place, she *was* huge and round and exhausted. And in the second place, she didn't want him to care about her.

At least that's what she told herself. He was exactly the kind of man she didn't need.

"So stop your fancying," Faith could hear her grandmother say.

"Thanks, Gram," she whispered. That's all it was. Fancying. Dreaming. Playing "let's pretend."

She swung her legs off the bed and started to get up, but another deep ache began in her lower abdomen and back. "Oh, no," she whispered. "Not yet, Li'l Bit. It's not time."

She flopped back down on the bed, huffing, just as Matt came back into the room. "Another contraction?" he asked and looked at his watch. "Eight minutes apart. We'd better get going."

"Eight minutes? That's impossible," she panted. "I'm not in labor."

Matt sat down beside her. "Faith, be quiet and listen to me. When my dad left, my mom was pregnant with my twin sisters. So trust me, I know all the signs. Plus while I was overseas, I had to deliver a baby for a woman in one of the villages we passed through."

Faith stared at him in horror. "Well, you're not delivering this one," she cried. "Call Glo!"

"It's okay. We've got time to get you to the hospital if we hurry."

"No!" she panted. The very idea of Matt seeing her... "No! Get Glo! Now!"

Matt's eyes widened. "Faith, don't worry—"

"Glo!" she screamed. "Glo!"

"Okay!" Matt shot up off the bed, his eyes wide and panicked. "Okay. She ought to be getting here about now. I'll get her."

He whirled and headed for the door just as, to Faith's

relief, Glo appeared. She'd apparently rushed right up. She didn't even have on her apron.

"Honey, what's going on here?" she said, rushing to Faith. "Good golly! You're about to have that baby."

"Why didn't you call me?" she snapped at Matt.

"I just..." he started.

"Get him out of here," Faith cried, almost doubled over with a contraction. "I don't care how many babies he's delivered. He's not going to deliver mine!"

She didn't catch what Glo said to Matt, but she heard him clomping down the stairs. Glo found her a robe and shoes and somehow got her downstairs and into the backseat of her car and climbed in with her. Matt was in the driver's seat.

As Matt burned rubber out of the café's parking lot and headed toward Holy Cross Hospital, Faith's contractions finally let up.

"Glo, thank God. You won't leave me, will you?"

"No, honey. Of course not. I'll be right there."

"Oh, no! Glo! It's Sunday! Who's going to help Valerio with the after-church lunch crowd?" she wailed.

"You don't worry about that. Matt'll help Valerio," Glo said sweetly. Then she poked Matt's shoulder with a finger.

"Won'tcha, hon?"

MATT WAS EXHAUSTED, his damn leg hurt like a son of a bitch and the only thing he'd eaten all day was a couple of mouthfuls of cherry pie after the Sunday post-church lunch crowd thinned out. Taking quick measure of the café's dining area, he figured he must have walked ten miles, if not more, taking orders, pouring coffee and bussing tables.

He already respected Faith for handling a business alone. From what he knew about her and her grandmother, he figured she couldn't be more than twenty-five or twenty-six. Now he was in total awe of her. She was the first one up every morning, and she closed the café every night. That made for a fifteen-hour day. *And* she was pregnant.

He picked up the last tableful of dirty dishes and wove his way through tables full of flowers and plants and baskets of baby things into the kitchen where Valerio was loading the industrial-sized dishwasher. "Aw, man," Valerio said. "I thought we were done."

Matt set the bin of dishes down with a groan. "It looks to me like you're never done around here."

"That's the truth," Molly said. She was sitting on a stool, polishing glasses with a snow-white cloth. Her hair was twisted up in a messy knot on top of her head, and she looked like she'd been up all night studying—or partying.

Valerio laughed. "That's how it feels, too." He turned on the dishwasher, then threw a towel across one shoulder and leaned against the counter.

"That was some crowd today, eh?" he said as he picked up his seemingly bottomless mug of coffee and took a swig.

"I thought it was just me, since I'm not used to working in a restaurant. I think I walked ten miles. This bum knee of mine is complaining."

"Glo claims a full day here is at least fifteen miles," Molly said.

Valerio nodded. "But no. This wasn't a typical Sunday. I think everybody in town showed up to talk about the shooting and find out about Faith's baby."

"I'll bet I was asked fifty times how she was doing and if she'd had the baby yet. And what's with all the flowers and baskets and things?"

"You never lived in a small town?" Without waiting for Matt's answer, Valerio went on. "Any time anything happens, everybody rallies around. Usually the casseroles and pies come out, too."

Matt frowned. "Casseroles and pies?"

"When someone is sick or dies or has a baby, the people of Freedom gather round. They take care of their own. Only, this being a café, and Faith being the best pie maker in town, I guess they don't want to bring food, so they all sent flowers and baskets."

Molly laughed. "I'll bet she's got this many at the hospital, too."

The idea was nearly incomprehensible to Matt. His idea of community was very different. The area of Los Angeles where he'd grown up had swarmed with gangs, and their rivalry made the streets a battleground. For Matt and his family, the person in the next apartment wasn't usually a friend. He was a potential threat.

He remembered the day he brought his mother home from the hospital after she'd had the twins. He'd barely turned thirteen and had begged a ride from a sympathetic nurse who was getting off duty around that time. Otherwise they'd have had to take the bus.

The only thing that greeted them at their apartment was the smell of rotting garbage and urine in the hallway. It was at that moment that Matt vowed he'd get his mother and sisters away from there.

Now he'd made good on that oath. He'd used the advance from Bart Bellows to move them to Amarillo. It was a move of faith. If his job with Bellows didn't work out, he'd have to figure out a way to support them, since he'd uprooted them from their homes, jobs and friends.

The phone rang, startling Matt's thoughts back to the present.

"Hola," Valerio said, then after a couple of seconds. *"Epa! Epa!* That's great."

Matt waited with bated breath. Was that Glo? Was Valerio so excited because Faith's baby had come? He bit his tongue, waiting for Valerio to finish talking.

"No, no. Stay. We're just fine here." After a couple more monosyllabic answers, Valerio turned to them. His dark face was alight with excitement.

Matt's heart thumped against his chest. "Valerio? Tell me. Was that Glo? Is Faith all right?"

"It's a girl!" Valerio cried. "Five pounds, nine and a half ounces."

"Wahoo!" Molly shouted. "A girl! Yes!" She pumped a fist in the air.

A girl. Faith was going to be so happy. She'd known she was having a girl.

"Is she…are they okay?" Matt looked down at his hand. It was shaking. He remembered how scary it had been when his mother had gone to the hospital to have his twin baby sisters. But for his mother, it was her fourth pregnancy. This was Faith's first, and it had been brought on by a traumatic event.

"Glori-ah says Faith is tired, but she's fine. And the baby *es muy hermosa*."

Beautiful. Of course the baby was beautiful. She had a beautiful mother.

"Do you think I can go see her?"

Valerio asked Glo, listened, said okay and hung up.

"Glori-ah thinks she should rest tonight. Why don't you go tomorrow morning? The café'll be closed, and Molly and I can handle cleaning and restocking."

Matt shook his head automatically. "What about you? Don't you want to see the baby? You've been here almost 24/7 this whole week."

Valerio looked sidelong at Matt. "Somehow, I think Faith will be happier to see you than me."

BEFORE HE WENT TO THE HOSPITAL, Matt went by his apartment to put a final coat of varnish on the crib. It looked spectacular. He'd hoped to finish painting her nursery for her, too, but he had no idea how long she'd be in the hospital. His mother had stayed for three days after having the twins, but that had been seventeen years ago.

At the hospital, after asking directions to Faith's room, he stopped in the gift shop and bought a single white calla lily in a long, slender vase.

When he got to the door of her room, his hands were shaking worse than ever, and his heart was pounding. The only time he could remember feeling like this was on his first date. That night hadn't gone well. He'd tried to kiss Esme Santos, and instead, he'd spilled a soft drink on her.

Damn, he hoped he could get through this without spilling something.

The door was ajar, so he knocked on it, then pushed it open and stepped inside.

And stared.

Faith, in a white nightgown trimmed with lace, was sitting up in a chair beside the bed. A patch of late afternoon sunlight shone through the window, surrounding her with a pale pinkish glow.

She was holding the baby, who had on a little pink cap and was waving her arms. Faith looked up and smiled. "Hi," she said.

Matt swallowed. "Hi. How're you doing?"

"I'm good. Really good. I was tired last night, but I slept well."

The baby gurgled, and Faith's attention returned immediately to her. She picked up the corner of a cloth and wiped the baby's mouth.

Matt was mesmerized. Faith looked like a blond Madonna, sitting in the light cast by the sunset. An ache throbbed in his chest, and absently, he rubbed it, but it didn't go away.

Faith touched the baby's nose with the tip of her forefinger and said something Matt didn't catch. The look on her face was unmistakable. It was a look of unconditional love of joy and wonder and amazement.

God help him, he couldn't take his eyes off her. And no amount of massage was going to lessen the ache in his chest. He had a feeling there was only one thing that would stop it. A pang of sheer terror shot through him.

"Matt?"

He blinked and met Faith's gaze. "Huh? I mean, where's Glo?"

"I made her go home last night. She wasn't happy about it, but she hadn't even left the room to eat since we got here. She said she was going to run by the café this morning to see if Valerio needed any help.

He nodded, unable to take his eyes off her.

She laughed. "Come and meet Kaleigh."

"Callie?"

She shook her head. "Kay-lee. I'm spelling it K-A-L-E-I-G-H."

He stepped cautiously over to her chair and looked down at the baby. "That's an awfully big name for such a tiny thing."

Faith touched Kaleigh's little hand with her finger, and the baby wrapped her minuscule fingers around it. Faith wriggled her finger a little, and Kaleigh held on.

"Kaleigh, sweetheart, I want you to meet a very nice man." She bent her head and kissed Kaleigh's tiny fingers. "Yes, I do, you precious little thing. This is Matt Soarez. He's my own personal knight, rescuing me from dragons and the governor's bodyguards."

Matt's dry throat suddenly felt scorched. He wanted to protest her description of him. But somewhere, deep inside, he felt the birth of a different emotion, the latest in a series of emotions he'd never felt before. He rubbed his chest again. The ache was still there, accompanied by pride, determination, responsibility and something he didn't recognize and couldn't put a name to.

Couldn't or wouldn't?

He sucked in a deep breath and tried to concentrate on Kaleigh rather than his mixed-up feelings. Then he remembered the vase in his hand. "I—I brought you something. That is, you and the baby."

At that instant, his brain processed what his eyes had seen when he'd first come into the room. Every surface was covered with baskets of flowers, stuffed animals and plants.

"Oh, Matt. It's lovely. Did someone tell you how much I love calla lilies? Thank you."

"I thought it was pretty, but next to all this—" he

swept his arm in a large arc "—my single flower looks pretty lame."

"No, it doesn't," Faith protested.

"Who sent all these?" he asked, eyeing the largest basket, which looked like it could hold his laundry for a month. It overflowed with boxes and jars of baby items and was topped with a pink stuffed bear that was at least three times Kaleigh's size.

"That came early this morning from the governor, with a note expressing regret that I was hurt because of her."

"And the rest?"

"The spray of carnations there is from the church. The Kemps sent the cute little basket there, and—" she stopped, shaking her head "—oh, there are too many. I can't remember who sent them all."

Kaleigh gave a minuscule hiccup, and Faith lifted her to her shoulder and gently patted her back.

Matt took a quick inventory of all the flowers. "The Hales," he said, peering at a card that came with a pothos plant. "Mayor Arkwright sent the yellow ones in the baby chick vase."

"That's right," Faith said. "Glo was starting to make a list for me before she left. She wanted to get to the café. Said Valerio and Molly would have wrecked the place by now."

"And me?" Matt asked, looking at her sidelong.

Faith blushed. "Well, you know how Glo is," she said, chuckling.

Matt grinned.

At that moment a brief knock sounded on the door.

"Oh, no. I'll bet they're coming to get the baby and take her back to the nursery," Faith said sadly.

But the head that poked around the edge of the door wasn't the nurse. It was Stockett.

"Hey, babe!" Stockett said, pushing the door open. He was holding a small stuffed bear with a pink ribbon around its neck.

Matt tensed but didn't move from his position on the other side of the room. He silently rose to the balls of his feet, readying himself for action, in case he needed to step between Stockett and Faith.

"Rory? What are you doing here?" Faith asked, an edge of fear in her voice.

Stockett's brows lowered, although he kept a smile pasted on his face. "Why, I came to see my baby. What have we got there? A girl?" He moved farther into the room, still apparently not noticing Matt.

"What a cutie. Look. She's got my nose. She's going to be a daddy's girl. Aren't you, princess?" He reached out a finger to touch Kaleigh's nose, and Faith recoiled.

"Don't touch her," she growled. "Ever!"

Stockett aimed his finger toward Faith's face. "Now you listen to me, Faith. I'm the father of that kid, and you can't keep me from seeing it. I've got a right."

Faith blinked, then cut her eyes over at Matt.

He'd already decided it was time to step in, so he took one long stride and ended up toe-to-toe with Stockett.

"Faith doesn't want you here," he said evenly.

"Aw, crap!" Stockett said. "You again? What the hell are you anyway, her private bodyguard?"

"Something like that."

Stockett's gaze flicked toward Faith then back to Matt. His face went dark with anger. "So that's how it is." He threw the stuffed bear down on the bed and turned, his hands doubling into fists.

"Rory, stop it!" Faith cried.

"You son of a bitch," Stockett roared. "How dare you touch her. She's mine. And so is that kid."

"Well, Stockett, that's the thing," Matt said easily, making no visible move to defend himself. He knew though, from past experience with Stockett as well as from his understanding of his own body, that he could get in at least two blows before Stockett got one. But he wanted to avoid that.

For one thing, it wouldn't be polite to fight in the Labor and Delivery wing of the hospital. For another, the room was too small, and he didn't want to take the chance of Faith and the baby getting caught in the fray.

Stockett's face was turning red. "What's the thing?"

"See, Faith can fill out the birth certificate any way she wants to. So she left the father's name blank." Matt shook his head in an attitude of regret. "So no. I hate to break it to you, but you're not the father."

"You mother—" Stockett punctuated his outburst with a right hook, but Matt caught his fist in one hand and placed his other hand on his bicep and twisted. He didn't jerk Stockett's arm around his back, but he showed him a taste of how it would feel if he had.

"Let's not have a scene here in the hospital, what do you say? If you insist, Faith will have to call security, and she'll have to charge you with disturbing the peace and attempted assault."

Stockett's red face was leaning toward purple, and his eyes bulged, showing white all the way around the irises. He tried one last move, shoving his weight against Matt.

Matt stepped back and let go of Stockett's arm. It was a risk, but from what he knew about the other man, he was pretty sure he didn't want a run-in with the police.

Stockett's face turned dark red, and he stuck out his chin pugnaciously. "I don't know who you think you are, *Señor Soarez,*" he said sarcastically, "but you and me, we're not done. You picked the wrong guy to mess with."

Matt didn't move. He just allowed his lips to curl up in a small smile.

"This is *not* the end of this!" Stockett yelled, jabbing a finger at Matt as he backed toward the door. "You and me have got a score to settle. So you better watch your back!"

Matt thought Stockett might do well to take his own advice. He watched in amusement as the other man backed toward a large nurse who had probably been a colonel in the army before she'd taken a job here. She'd silently stepped through the door just about the time Stockett said, "wrong guy."

"Hey!" she barked.

Stockett nearly fell over his feet.

"This is a hospital," she continued in her clipped military tone, "and you're disturbing the peace. Shall I call security, mister? Or will you be going?"

With a glance back at Faith and a glare for Matt, Stockett slinked out the door like a kitten sneaking around the neighborhood's top cat.

Once he was gone, the nurse dusted her hands and smiled at Faith. Matt was intrigued by the instantaneous change in her. Now the large and in charge military nurse looked like a grandmother.

"Time for Kaleigh to rest," she said gently and took Kaleigh from Faith's arms. "And time for Mommy to rest, too."

She turned and looked at Matt. "I hope you're going to take care of that two-bit grifter," she said sternly. "If he shows up here again, I'll call the sheriff."

Matt nodded.

The nurse left, cooing down at Kaleigh.

Faith's wide blue eyes searched Matt's. "How did you know about the birth certificate?" she asked.

"Glo told me that's what you were planning to do." Matt paused for an instant. "When will they let you and the baby go home?"

"I can go tomorrow if I think I'm ready."

"Tomorrow?" If Matt wanted to get the nursery painted, it would have to be tonight.

"I'm still a little unsure about how to—" her hand went to her breast, and her cheeks flamed.

"How to—?" Matt asked, then he realized what she meant and he felt his face heat up, too. "Don't worry," he said. "I'm pretty sure Kaleigh will figure it out."

He picked up the stuffed bear that Stockett brought. "You want this?"

Faith shook her head without taking her gaze from Matt's. "No! I don't want anything from him. And I don't want him around Kaleigh." She took a shaky breath. "What if he comes back? What am I going to do?"

Stockett's last words rang in Matt's ears. *Score to settle. Watch your back.* "Don't worry about it. I think

Stockett's going to run into somebody his own size one of these days."

Matt just hoped he could keep Faith safe until he could make sure Stockett wouldn't bother her again.

Chapter Eleven

Faith's doctor was tied up in an emergency the next day, so it was Wednesday before Faith and Kaleigh came home from the hospital.

This gave Matt enough time to paint the nursery and bring the crib in. He moved the rocking chair and a side table in from the living room. Glo brought up all the baskets and flowers that had been sent to the café.

When Faith saw the nursery and the crib, she burst into tears, which surprised Matt.

"Hey," he said. "This is supposed to be a good thing—a gift for you and Kaleigh."

"It's—so—beautiful," she sobbed. "I can't take it all in. Where did the crib come from?"

"I brought it from my mom's house," Matt said. "She said to tell you that it held five well-loved babies. She said your baby will be blessed."

"He refinished it himself," Glo added.

Faith cried even harder. Glo put her arm around her and led her to the rocking chair. "Sit, hon, and enjoy your room. Matt's got to go, don't you?"

Matt got the message. "Yep. I've got a lot to do." He sent Glo a meaningful look. "Take care of them," he said.

He headed downstairs and over to the courthouse, looking for the sheriff. He wanted to see the media footage of the town hall meeting.

Forty minutes and three tapes later, Sheriff Hale leaned back in his ancient wooden desk chair. "And that's it," he said.

Matt, who'd propped a hip on the edge of the sheriff's desk, shook his head. "Not much. That's for sure."

Hale pointed the remote at the TV and turned off the image. "Yeah. Luckily the networks wanted as much footage of the governor as they could get. Of course they all want the exclusive when we find the guy who did the shooting."

"Can we run through them again?"

"Sure." The sheriff tossed the remote to Matt. "You go ahead and more power to you if you can spot something I've missed. I've been through them twice already, and all I can see is that baseball cap. Once the gunshot is fired, it's utter chaos."

"I'd like to take them with me if I can. I want to get back and check on Faith and the baby."

Hale nodded. "She's out of the hospital now, isn't she? I never did get by to see her. She doing okay? And the baby?"

"They're doing great. The baby is beautiful."

Hale's dark eyes scrutinized Matt. "You've been a big help to Faith," he said pointedly.

Matt felt a flush beginning to heat his cheeks. "I had to hang out at the diner anyway, and with Stockett back in the area Faith needed someone around."

"Uh-huh," Hale muttered, then gestured toward the TV. "Take all three of the disks. I hope you can spot something."

Matt gathered them. "I'll take good care of these," he said.

"You sure as hell will," Hale responded, reaching into his bottom desk drawer and pulling out a form. "This is a form for receipt of police evidence. Failing to return such evidence costs a fine of five hundred dollars for each piece plus possible jail time, depending on the importance of the information contained on the aforementioned disks."

"Yes, sir." Matt dutifully signed the forms and handed them back to the sheriff. "What about the crime scene investigators? Did they turn up anything?"

"They found the baseball cap. It'd been kicked up under the lunch counter, and it was trampled, but still intact—for the most part. Probably no chance of getting a fingerprint."

"Or DNA?"

"Doesn't look good. We've got the bullet, though."

Matt frowned. "Damn it, Sheriff, you could have told me that say—" he looked at his watch "—an hour ago when I first walked in here."

"And the cartridge. Although it was trampled, too."

"The cartridge, too? How long were you planning to hold on to this news?"

"Till just about now." Sheriff Hale sat up and Matt saw the glint of excitement in his eyes. "The bullet was under the makeshift stage, just like I figured it'd be. After it went through the bodyguard, it didn't have enough momentum to stick in the wall."

"What is it? What does CSI say about it?"

"It's from a 9 mm," the sheriff said, watching Matt. "But get this. The cartridge was crushed, but the team managed to read what was on the headstamp. Here's what it looks like." Hale drew a circle and filled in letters and numbers.

"There," Matt said, pointing. "That *03* printed right there? That's the date the cartridge was manufactured. That means it's military issue!" Matt blew out his breath in a whoosh.

"Whoever this guy is, he's got connections. It's possible for a civilian to get those, but it's not easy."

"The crime scene boys are seeing if they can lift a print off the cartridge, and my men are combing the area right around town in case he dropped the gun as he ran."

"Damn it. He was tall, with that baseball cap on. He could be ex-military, and he was carrying. I should have been able to pick him out of the crowd. Hell, I should have smelled him," Matt said disgustedly.

"Come on, Matt. Don't beat yourself up. There was no way we could keep up with every single person in the crowd."

"Well, if there's anything on those surveillance disks, I'm going to find it."

"I sure hope so," Hale said. He pulled a file folder toward him and opened it as Matt headed out the door.

Back at the café, he started up the stairs and met Glo coming down. "There you are. Valerio just got a delivery of several cases of chicken. He could use some help getting it out of the van and hauling it down to the basement freezer."

"How's Faith doing? And the baby?"

"They're both fine."

"I'll just run up—"

Glo put out a hand. "You'll just go help Valerio. Faith's feeding Kaleigh."

His face burning with embarrassment, he turned around on the stairs. "Yes, ma'am."

It took Matt and Valerio three trips through the kitchen, across the café's dining room and down the stairs to the basement to finish storing the meat in the big freezer chest.

Matt sat down on a chair in the basement and mopped his forehead. "How do you do it?"

Valerio grinned at Matt and flexed his biceps. "Takes me twice as long by myself, but it's good exercise."

"You got that right. Too bad this basement isn't a walk-out," Matt said. "It sure would help if you could drive around and bring the stuff straight in." He looked around. The basement was well lit and equipped with an industrial-sized freezer that took up one entire wall, a bank of heavy steel shelves where canned goods were stored and a large metal safe, complete with a numbered dial.

"I worked in a couple of restaurants growing up," Matt went on, "and this is one of the neatest storerooms I've ever seen. But I gotta ask, how in hell did Faith get that monster of a freezer down here? And what's that?" He pointed to a large metal safe, complete with a numbered dial.

"Just what it looks like."

"What it looks like is that Faith could open her own bank. Where did it come from, and how did it get down here?"

"Can't tell you that. The safe and the freezer have been here as long as I've worked here, and I started working for Faith's *abuela*, Señora Eliza, fifteen years ago." Valerio sighed. "I'd retired from the air force, and my wife died soon after, leaving me with two boys."

"Two boys," Matt repeated. "What ages?"

"They were four and six months when their mother died. Sonny is nineteen now, and Carlos is almost sixteen." Valerio's black eyes lit up as he talked about his boys.

"That's great. I'd like to meet them."

"You should. You should," he said.

"So you started working for Faith's grandmother back then. Faith has told me about her. She died a couple of years ago, right?"

Valerio nodded.

"What about her mother—and her dad?"

Valerio picked up a case of ketchup and headed up the basement stairs. "Grab that case of mayonnaise," he told Matt. "We're about out again."

Matt hoisted the case and followed Valerio. When they got upstairs and set down their loads, Valerio turned to Matt.

"From what I've heard, Eliza and William Scott lived in this house for many years. Eliza made the downstairs into a café after William died around 1968 or 1967. Faith's mom would have been around six or so. I started working for Señora Eliza around 1980, just about the time Mary left. Six years later, she returned, pregnant with Faith."

"What about Faith's father?" Matt asked, fearing he knew the answer.

"Never saw hide nor hair of him. Word was that he was a drifter. He showed up in town, Faith's mother fell head over heels in love and followed him."

There it was. Yet another reason for Faith not to trust

him. Not only was her first serious relationship with a drifter, a con man and a liar but her mother's had been, too.

At this point, even if Matt told Faith who he really was, she'd probably feel doubly betrayed. There was no way she'd ever—Matt shook his head, trying to dislodge the thought that almost made it into his conscious brain.

"Que pasa, amigo?" Valerio said. "Got a headache or something?"

"What?" Matt asked, then realized what Valerio meant. "No. Just thinking about something. So is there anything else you need right now?"

Valerio eyed him closely. "Not as bad as you need to check on Faith," he said.

"I just thought I'd look in on her. Then I've got something I need to do." He picked up the disks from the counter where he'd left them while he was helping Valerio, left the kitchen and headed for the stairs.

As soon as he made sure Faith and the baby were settled in, he was going to go to his apartment and study the footage. Somewhere on one of the disks was the shooter, and Matt intended to find him.

FAITH SNUGGLED BACK AGAINST the mound of pillows Glo had surrounded her with and looked down at Kaleigh, who'd just finished drinking her fill. Now she was waving her arms and screwing her face up into a little scowl.

"Your little tummy is full now, isn't it little girl? Yes it is. You need to burp, Kaleigh?" Faith murmured. "Is that what's bothering you? Hmm?"

She lifted her and placed her against her left shoulder

and patted her back. As she tapped lightly on Kaleigh's back, she pressed her cheek against her daughter's impossibly soft skin. The feel of the precious cheek against hers sent a wave of emotion through her that she'd never felt before. It was partly thrilling, partly terrifying and overlaid with a depth of love that even twenty-four hours ago Faith would have said was impossible. Nobody could love that much.

But she knew better now. She did love Kaleigh that much—that much and more. A lump grew in her throat, and tears pricked her eyes.

"Hey, Kaleigh. Hey, baby," she whispered as she patted the baby's back. "Me and you, we're going to do just fine, aren't we?" She was rewarded with a fairly loud belch.

"Ooh, that was a good one," she chuckled. "Who knew such a dainty little lady could belch like that?" She lay Kaleigh back down in her arm and took the edge of the burping cloth and wiped her little mouth.

"There you go," she said. "That's a good girl." Faith closed her eyes, just for a minute, and hummed a wordless lullaby that her mother had sung to her when she was little.

"It's you and me, Kaleigh," she said softly, moving the baby gently back and forth in a rocking motion. "Just you and me. We don't need anybody, do we? Especially a man." Faith felt sadness push its way into her heart at those words. "We can make it on our own, can't we, sweetie?"

MATT MADE IT TO THE DOOR of Faith's bedroom in time to hear her say "especially a man. We can make it on our own, can't we, sweetie?"

The words cut a deep gash into a section of his heart he hadn't even realized was there. He knew it now, though, because it hurt like hell. For a second, he hesitated, wondering if he should come back later. He *really* didn't want to interrupt Faith's sweet, intimate moment with her child.

"Glo? Matt? Who's out there?"

That did it. She'd heard him. "It's me," he said, stepping around the door facing and pasting a big smile on his face. The sight before him completely shattered the smile and filled up his heart with longing.

Faith was sitting up in bed in a pale blue gown, holding Kaleigh in her arms. Her pale blond hair was braided, but wisps and tendrils had escaped and were waving around her face, which glowed with happiness and serenity.

"Hi," she said, smiling at him.

Matt swallowed and tried to speak, but his throat was closed up. Not only was he acting like a teenager in the throes of his first crush but he was experiencing a whole different set of emotions that threw him back in time by seventeen years, when his mom brought the twin baby girls home from the hospital.

He'd known from the first moment he saw his baby sisters that he wanted to be a father. He loved babies. They were so sweet when they were infants. And every day was a new discovery, a new adventure from finding their fingers and toes to their first word to their first steps and on and on and on.

"Matt? Is everything all right?" Faith's brows drew down into a frown.

"Sure," he croaked, then cleared his throat. "Sure.

Everything's fine. I just wanted to check on you. Make sure you got settled in okay."

"Glo took really good care of me." Faith shifted in the bed.

"What's the matter?" Matt asked.

"It's nothing. I'd like to put Kaleigh down for a nap, but my gown is twisted, and I don't want to disturb her by moving around too much. She's asleep." Faith looked down at her baby then up at Matt.

The love scripted on her beautiful face took Matt's breath away. "I could—" he started, then cleared his throat again "—I'll take her. I can put her in the bassinet for you."

Faith lifted her chin and stared into Matt's eyes. "Can you?"

"Sure," he said. "Remember, I told you about my twin baby sisters? I took care of them from the minute they came home from the hospital. You could ask my mom. I'm great with newborns and one-year-olds, and toddlers—" He stopped when Faith's eyes widened and then she blinked.

He shouldn't have said that. He'd gone too far, implying he'd be around when Kaleigh was a year old or even two.

"That's, um, good," Faith said uncertainly. "So you know you have to support her head, right?"

Matt leaned over to slide his hand under Kaleigh's head, which put him within kissing distance of Faith's mouth. To his chagrin and sudden discomfort, he actually thought about it for a second.

Faith's eyes were downcast, watching the baby. Her long, pale lashes shaded her eyes, and one of the wisps of hair that had escaped her braid tickled his nose. But before he lost his head, not to mention control of a certain portion of his anatomy, he turned his thoughts back to the baby, whose fine, blond hair felt like angel's hair in his palm.

"Okay, Miss Kaleigh," he whispered. "Let's get you to bed for a nap. Your mommy needs to rest, too." He lifted the tiny bundle and set it in the crib. When he turned back to Faith, she was watching him with an odd expression on her face.

"There. See?" he said. "She's just fine."

Faith nodded. "I see," she said, her voice raspy.

Matt avoided her gaze by smoothing the bedspread and patting it. "Now you need to get some rest. I'm going to—"

"Stay," Faith murmured. "Stay here for a while."

"I—"

"Just while I take a nap. I mean, I don't want to keep you if you're busy. It's just that Glo's got to help Valerio with the cooking, and I'd rather have someone here. In the hospital, the nurses were always there. I'm terrified that if I go to sleep I won't hear Kaleigh crying."

Matt wanted to say, "trust me, you'll hear her. Those tiny lungs can wake the whole building." But when he looked at Faith, her eyes were closed and her lips were slightly parted.

She'd already gone to sleep.

For longer than he would ever admit, even to himself, he watched her sleep. Sitting there, beside her bed, watching as her chest rose and fell with each breath and her eyelids flickered with dreams, Matt finally admitted to himself what he had never dared to even think before.

He was falling in love with Faith. He was already

in love with Kaleigh. It had taken her no more than a second to wrap his heart around her tiny little finger.

It had taken longer with Faith. Or maybe it had just taken longer for him to admit it. The first time he'd ever seen her she'd taken his breath away. She'd glided out of the kitchen with a tray of full cups of coffee held at shoulder height. After she'd handed out the coffee she'd turned to him at the lunch counter and asked if he wanted some.

His throat had turned as dry as it was right now when she'd pinned him with her blue eyes and that small, shy smile.

And right now, with her lashes resting on her cheeks and her lips parted in sleep, she still stole his breath.

Oh, boy, he thought, exerting all his energy to resist touching her cheek. He was in big trouble.

Chapter Twelve

Matt didn't mind staying with Faith while she took a nap. It felt comfortable and somehow right to sit in the living room while Faith and Kaleigh slept.

He was watching the third and last disk of the footage from the town hall meeting when he heard Kaleigh whine. He jumped up and headed into the bedroom.

The baby was awake and gearing up to cry.

"Hey, Kaleigh," he whispered, darting a look over at Faith to be sure she was still asleep. "Let's go into the living room, okay? I'll rock you, and you can help me figure out which one of a hundred people on the TV is the bad guy. Okay?"

He picked up Kaleigh and felt her diaper to see if she was wet. She was. Still talking to her in a whisper, he carried her out to the living room and pulled the bedroom door behind him. On the floor by the door, he spotted a diaper bag, and using the coffee table, he made quick work of changing Kaleigh's diaper.

"There you go," he whispered close to her ear. "Now let's you and me watch some TV while Mommy sleeps."

Kaleigh started to whine again, so Matt put her

against his shoulder and patted her back until she burped.

Then he sat down in the wooden rocking chair and settled Kaleigh in his arm. He started up the DVD player again. He'd been watching the footage on Mute so it wouldn't wake Faith or the baby.

As the camera panned the crowd, many of whom he didn't know, but whose faces he was becoming familiar with, he leaned forward slightly. After watching two sets of footage of the same event, he recognized the farmer in his mid-sixties who was asking Governor Lockhart a question. The shot was about to be fired—in about five seconds.

With the sound off, all Matt saw was the reaction of the camera operator and the crowd. The camera wavered for a few seconds until the cameraman recovered from the shock of the gunshot. Then it straightened. By then, heads were ducking, some people were turning toward the sound of the shot and others had started pushing through the crowd.

From this camera's vantage point he saw a hand with a microphone go up, fall and then go up again.

Matt shook his head. "We were lucky no one was trampled, Kaleigh," he said. "Especially your mommy, although she almost was. That gunshot is why you're already here. I don't think you were scheduled to make your appearance for another four or five weeks.

"Watch," he told the infant. "In a minute, you'll see your mommy and you. Of course you'll be on the inside of your mommy instead of—" He paused as he watched the screen. He was seeing something he hadn't seen on the other two disks.

Instead of swerving the camera toward the stage and

the injured bodyguard, this cameraman swept the panicked crowd. He was obviously nervous, so the camera
wavered nauseatingly and swung much faster than
normal, but he did manage to pan the entire inside of
the diner before he focused on the front doors.

Matt sat up straight. There had to be at least a split
second of the shooter on that piece of film.

"Let's watch that again," he whispered to Kaleigh.
When he looked down, the big beautiful eyes were
closed and her tiny lips were parted. She looked just
like her mother. Matt bent his head and pressed a tender
kiss to the precious, brand-new forehead. Its softness
raised a lump in his throat.

"You are so beautiful," he murmured. "Just like your
mommy." He stood carefully and carried Kaleigh back
to her crib and laid her in it.

Her little brow knitted a bit, but then she went right
back into her deep sleep.

Matt pressed Rewind on the remote and waited several seconds before stopping it. Then he studied the
remote control, hoping to find a button that would run
the footage forward in slow motion. He didn't find one.
so he ran it again at regular speed.

This camera had been positioned closer to the stage
so that shots of the governor at the podium necessarily
included part of the crowd. Matt played the footage for
a few seconds then paused, studying the crowd, then
pressed Play again and repeated the sequence.

He saw the man in the blue baseball cap twice. Both
times the cap was pulled down low over his eyes, but the
second time, his head was lifted enough for Matt to see
a black mustache. He rewound and watched again, pressing Pause just as the baseball cap came into view.

Matt scrutinized the images on the screen from super-close, from midrange and from the other side of the room, but no position made the image any clearer. The only thing it gained for him was to verify what he remembered. The man was wearing an ordinary blue long-sleeved shirt, another generic item, like the cap, that could easily be shed. He could have had a T-shirt on underneath that would completely change his appearance.

He let the disk run, hoping the camera had stayed on the crowd long enough to record the man actually shooting the gun.

It hadn't. But Matt kept watching. Maybe he could catch a glimpse of the shooter after he'd dropped the cap. He'd give half a year's salary to be able to identify the man who'd tried to kill Governor Lockhart.

FAITH HEARD KALEIGH WHIMPER softly. She opened her eyes and checked her bedside clock. Six o'clock! She'd slept for two hours. She hadn't meant to nap more than a few minutes. Kaleigh would be wet and uncomfortable. Quickly, she got up and went over to the crib. Kaleigh was sleeping peacefully. Faith checked her for wetness, but she was dry, which was impossible after two hours, wasn't it?

Had Matt changed her? He must have. What an amazing man he was. He knew all about babies. He'd even delivered one while he was serving in Iraq. And, although he'd shown up in town from who-knew-where for a temporary construction job, as soon as the governor announced that she wanted to hold a town hall meeting in Freedom, he'd gotten involved in the security details, working with the sheriff. What else was there about him that she didn't know?

That thought, which should have worried her, given her and her mother's histories with handsome, charming drifters, actually warmed her. Getting to know more about Matt Soarez was something she'd love to do. As usual, the practical, rational side of her brain rose up to say, *No, you do not want or need to know more about him.*

This time though, her rational side didn't win. This time she allowed herself a few minutes to consider what life would be like with Matt. If he were what he said he was, just an itinerant worker in town for a job, then she should turn and run in the opposite direction. But if he was what he appeared to be maybe this time her heart wasn't wrong. Maybe this time she could have her happy ending.

Lost in thought, she wandered into the living room.

Matt's head turned, then he rose from the rocking chair. When his gaze met hers, his whole face lit up—or maybe it was a trick of the light. "Faith, you shouldn't be out of bed."

She smiled. "Yes, I should. Specific instructions from my obstetrician. He wants me sitting up and walking. And by the way, not napping for two hours in the middle of the day."

"You were exhausted. You needed the sleep."

"I didn't need that much sleep. Did you change her?"

"Yep. I told you I'm really good with newborns. I can do everything except feed 'em." He grinned, then blushed.

Faith felt her own cheeks heat up at the joke. Then

dismay flooded her. "I didn't hear her crying. Oh, how am I going to take care of her if I don't wake up when she cries?"

"Hey," Matt said, his grin fading to a warm smile, "as soon as I heard her moving around, I checked on her. She barely whimpered. I got her changed and then we rocked and watched some TV together until she went back to sleep. She's a good baby."

She nodded. "Thank you for taking care of her. I was pretty tired." She glanced at the TV. "What are you watching?"

"The networks' footage of the town hall meeting."

"Oh," she said. "I see. There's the governor." The picture on the TV screen was of a side shot of Lila Lockhart. She'd grabbed the microphone and come out from behind the podium to answer a woman's question.

"I remember this," she said, her heart pounding in reaction and memory. "Right after she stepped out in front of the podium, the guy shot at her."

Matt sent her a thoughtful look and paused the TV. "That's right. He waited until she'd come out from behind the lectern. Do you remember anything else specific?"

"No. I was terrified that I was going to get trampled by the crowd."

"You almost did. I should have been more careful about where I let you stand. If you hadn't gotten pushed into the wall by the governor's bodyguards, you might not have gone into labor."

Faith smiled. "Everything turned out okay, and from what a lot of the ladies in town tell me, I had a very easy delivery. So maybe at least that part of what happened was for the best."

Matt's dark eyes softened. "Maybe so. I'm sure glad I got to meet Kaleigh. If you'd gone full term, I probably wouldn't be here."

"Wouldn't be here?" His seemingly offhand comment almost stole her breath. "Are you? You're not leaving, are you?" she asked quickly.

"Not anytime soon," he answered, "but I have to follow the job."

"Oh, no. I know. Of course you do." Faith tried as hard as she could to make her voice sound young and happy and carefree. From the look on Matt's face, she'd failed. "You, uh, don't know where you'll go from here, then?"

Matt shook his head and turned his gaze back to the TV. He pressed Play.

She shouldn't have asked that. For one thing, it was none of her business. She scrambled for something to say. "Kaleigh's sleeping a lot. Do you think she's okay?"

He chuckled. "Be glad she's sleeping. Pretty soon you'll be up at all hours feeding her and walking the floor with her when she has a tummy ache."

His expression turned serious, and he reached out and pushed a strand of hair back behind her ear. "Stop worrying so much," he said softly. "You're going to be a wonderful mother, Faith. Trust me. I'm very good at reading people."

Can you read this? Faith thought. She smiled shyly and touched his hand, which was still lingering over the strand of hair he'd tucked.

Matt's fingers slid around the back of her neck, and he leaned down and kissed her, at first sweetly. But after a couple of seconds, his tongue touched her lips, and with a gasp, she parted them and closed her eyes. Matt's head dipped lower and he deepened the kiss.

Faith's body responded, surprising her. She'd wanted this, but she hadn't expected her sore, achy body to have such feelings as were coursing through her now.

He pulled her closer, wrapping his arms tenderly around her, and kept on kissing her. Then he traced the line of her jaw with his lips, searching for and finding her earlobe and nipping at it teasingly.

Her legs went weak, and a sweet, intense throbbing began deep within her. She craned her neck backward and pressed her full breasts against his chest.

He brought his mouth back to hers and kissed her long and thoroughly, his tongue sensually imitating the act of love.

Faith felt as if he'd stolen her breath totally. But his kisses were like breath to her—like life. She could survive as long as he kept kissing her.

Matt drew back, looking her in the eye, searching for something she couldn't identify. She stood on tiptoes and sought his mouth again. He pulled her to him, pressing her length against his. She felt his erection brush against her and felt her insides contract in a sudden spurt of desire.

"Mmm," she moaned, and Matt stopped.

"Did I hurt you?" he said, his brow furrowed.

"I'm just still sore," she whispered, shy about having to explain her accidental moan of pain.

She ducked her head and looked away, pressing her temple against his shoulder. Her gaze lit on the TV.

"Oh, my God!" she cried, pushing away from him.

Matt tensed and grabbed her shoulders. "Faith? What is it?"

She pointed at the screen. "I just remembered. I thought I'd seen Rory in all the chaos, but then the body-guards were rushing Governor Lockhart out and trying to help the guard that was shot, and I got pushed and I forgot all about him. Why would he be at the town hall meeting?"

"When did you first see him?"

Faith thought about it. "I think it was right after Henry yelled *liar.* Right about the time the gunshot rang out."

Within a split second, Matt had grabbed the remote and stopped the DVD. "Why did you think it was Stock-ett?" he asked.

Faith stared at the screen, which showed the governor frozen in time just as she leaned forward, her gaze on a man in the third row who was talking.

Tearing her gaze away from the film footage, she closed her eyes. "He was toward the back. He had on a blue shirt and a baseball cap."

Matt pressed Rewind, then started it again. "Okay. Watch and tell me when you spot him."

Faith watched. The camera panned the crowd, and then suddenly it wavered and people began ducking and shouting and pushing. Faith scanned the faces. Where was Rory? She'd been sure she'd seen him.

"Well?" Matt asked, a serious note in his voice.

"No. Maybe I was wrong. It was just a glimpse, and everything happened so fast once the gun went off. Maybe you should rewind a little further, back around the time Henry Kemp yelled *liar.*"

Matt rewound again.

Faith moved closer to the TV and watched intently. "There! Now Play."

She saw the figure that she'd thought was Rory. "That's why I saw him. He was standing behind Henry," she said, frowning at the screen. "But I don't know. Maybe it's not him. That guy looks like he has a mustache."

Matt's whole body went tense. "Where, Faith? Where is he?" He held out the remote. "You drive. Zero in on him."

Faith took the remote and worked the picture back and forth until she pinpointed the very instant Rory first appeared on the screen. "See? Right there?" She pointed, touching the screen with a finger. "He has a birthmark—a white patch of hair just behind his left ear."

Matt leaned forward, too, frowning. "I don't remember a white patch."

"It's right there." She touched the screen behind his ear. "You didn't notice it when you two met at the café or when you fought in the alley?"

Matt shook his head. "Go back, just a touch."

Faith manipulated the remote control buttons.

"Damn it."

Faith could feel the waves of tension coming from Matt. It wasn't much of a leap to figure out that he thought Rory could be the shooter. "What's wrong? You think Rory did it, don't you?"

Matt gave a quick shake of his head. "I don't know. It's possible. But I can't identify that man you're pointing out as Rory Stockett. Granted, I've only seen him twice. And what you're calling a white patch in his hair, well, I can't see that either." He sighed. "I do see the mustache though, so I think you've spotted our shooter.

The problem now is trying to make a positive ID, not to mention finding Stockett."

Faith swallowed hard. "Listen, Matt. I do not want to know that my baby's father may have tried to kill the governor, but I'm almost one hundred percent sure that *that* is Rory Stockett. The only reason it's not a full hundred percent is because of the mustache."

Matt narrowed his gaze, searching her face. She gave him back look for look until she heard Kaleigh fussing.

"She's hungry. I've got to feed her."

Matt nodded. "I need to show this to the sheriff, then I suspect we'll be taking it into Amarillo to see if their forensic photography department can clear up the picture enough to make a positive ID." He took back the remote as Faith went to pick up Kaleigh.

When she came back into the room, he had the disks in a plastic bag and was headed for the door.

"Matt?" she said tentatively.

He turned.

"I'll do anything I can to help. I have no illusions about Rory."

Matt's wide mouth was grim. "Have you got any pictures of him?"

She shook her head. "No. He never liked having his picture taken."

Matt's expression telegraphed his opinion of why that was.

"Well, then, I'm pretty sure you're going to have to describe him to a police artist. I'll get Sheriff Hale to set that up."

Faith nodded as she patted Kaleigh's back, but Kaleigh wasn't satisfied with patting. She was hungry, and she told Faith so in the only way she knew how—by crying.

"Matt?" Faith said again, over Kaleigh's cries. "I hope you—" she stopped. Whatever she'd thought about saying, she couldn't. So she ended lamely, "You'll let me know, won't you? About Rory?"

Matt's chin lifted, and one corner of his mouth turned up in a wry smile. "Don't worry," he said. "It would be my pleasure to lock up your boyfriend for this shooting."

Chapter Thirteen

It was the next afternoon before Matt and Sheriff Hale could see Bart Bellows to update him on the shooting.

Bellows sat behind his desk and scrutinized the enlarged photo of the cartridge's headstamp. "It does look like military issue. What about the gun?"

"My chief deputy, Jeff Appleton, found it yesterday afternoon. He and my other deputies have been Dumpster diving ever since Saturday night."

Matt had already heard about the gun from the sheriff, but he was still excited about the find. If the shooter had tossed it down a storm drain or found a pond or lake to throw it into, they might never have retrieved it.

"What Appleton found was a 9 mm Beretta," the sheriff told Bellows. "It was wrapped in a blue shirt, the kind that can be bought anywhere. No fingerprints. I've sent the weapon and the shirt by courier to the forensics lab in Amarillo to see if the gun and bullet's markings are the same."

"Good. I'll let the commissioner know and ask him to make that top priority. He's as concerned about the governor's safety as we are." Bellows frowned. "Did you see anything on the shirt? Hairs? Sweat?"

Hale shook his head. "I hope the lab can pick up something."

Bellows turned his attention to Matt. It would be pushing it to say he was amused, but there was a hint of a twinkle in his eye. "You're about to burst, son. What's your news?"

Matt took a deep breath. "We may have footage of the shooter, sir."

Bellows didn't speak. He waited for Matt to go on.

"Faith—Ms. Scott—thought she caught a glimpse of Rory Stockett right after the shooting." Matt paused when he saw Bellows's eyebrows go up.

"Well? Go on," Bellows said. "How does Ms. Scott's baby daddy figure into all this?"

Matt explained. "She was watching the footage of the meeting with me. She pointed out the man she believes is Stockett. He's not wearing a baseball cap, so if he's the shooter, he'd already dropped it by then. But he does seem to have a mustache, which would have to be false. He didn't have one the other day."

"So she believes the man on the tape is Stockett? If she was involved with him and she's not sure it's him, how does that help us?" Bellows asked.

Matt sat forward and rested his elbows on his knees. "There's one more thing, sir. Stockett has a birthmark, a white patch of hair behind his left ear. Ms. Scott believes she can see the white patch on the mustached man on the disk."

Bellows leaned back in his wheelchair and tented his fingers. "Where's that footage?" he asked.

"We've sent the original disk the network gave us to Amarillo, to see if the shot of the man can be enlarged and enhanced. But we have a copy if you'd like to see it."

"Bah," Bellows said. "I have no reason to look at a grainy picture of a man who might or might not be our shooter. That's why I hire professionals. What's your next move, Sheriff?"

Hale scratched his chin. "We've put out an APB on Stockett. The only photo we have of him is the DMV photo for his driver's license. But his license is up for renewal, so that picture is almost six years old."

"You mean Faith Scott doesn't have a picture of him?" Bellows asked Matt.

"No, sir. Apparently Stockett didn't like to have his picture taken."

"Makes sense." He turned back to Hale. "So you've notified airports, bus stations, all that?"

Hale nodded. "I doubt it's going to do any good. I'm betting he's laying low right around here somewhere."

"What about the girl? Ten to one she knows how to contact him."

"No, sir," Matt protested. "She doesn't want anything to do with him."

Bellows looked Matt square in the eye. "He's the father of her baby, son."

Matt lowered his gaze. Bellows was right. Matt could believe anything he wanted about Faith, but he'd only known her for a matter of days. In reality, he had no idea if she knew how to contact Stockett. It occurred to him that he hadn't asked her.

"Have you questioned her?" Bellows asked the sheriff, as if he'd read Matt's mind.

"She's working with a forensic artist who's using the

DMV shot plus her description to get a current likeness of him."

"Get her in for questioning. I'll guarantee you she knows something."

"She just had a baby, sir," Matt objected before he could stop himself. He should have bitten his tongue. His number one priority was Governor Lockhart's safety, not Faith's.

Bellows pinned him with his sharp eyes. "I'm aware of that, but this is a matter of life and death for Lila Lockhart. She needs to be questioned."

It took a lot of determination for Matt not to duck his head. "Yes, sir."

"And not by you, Bernie. I'll have the chief of police in Amarillo send a policewoman to question Ms. Scott. Meanwhile—" Bellows turned back to Matt, pointing a finger at him "—you contact that muscle head who collected on her loan. Somebody knows where Stockett is. If he's the one who pulled that trigger, I want him behind bars *now!*"

FAITH SHIFTED KALEIGH TO HER left arm and nodded miserably at the policewoman who'd just introduced herself as Detective Mary Anne Ingram with the Amarillo Police Department.

"Come in," Faith said, stepping back to let the detective into her apartment.

"What an adorable baby," Detective Ingram cooed. "Did you want to put her down for a nap while we talk?"

To Faith, the question sounded more like an order. She lifted Kaleigh to her shoulder one more time and patted her back. She was rewarded with a tiny belch.

Detective Ingram chuckled. "How cute," she said. "I don't have kids yet. Trying to get established. You know, get a few years under my belt, before I even think about starting a family."

Faith laid Kaleigh in her crib and came back into the living room. She picked up the sheet and pillow off the couch. "Please, sit down."

Detective Ingram eyed the bed clothes. "Got a friend staying over I see."

Faith bit her lip. She hadn't had a chance to talk to Matt after he and Sheriff Hale had left that morning. Was this what they'd been doing? Setting up an interrogation of *her* with the Amarillo P.D.? He could have called and warned her.

Or maybe not. Maybe there was some law or regulation that had prevented him from telling her that she was about to be questioned.

"Would you like some water, Detective?"

"No, no. I'm fine." The policewoman took a small digital recorder off her uniform belt and set it on the coffee table between them. "I'll be recording our interview. For the record."

Faith nodded again. She licked her lips and swallowed with difficulty. She wished she had some water.

"Now," Ingram said, "you are the sole owner of the Talk of the Town Café?"

"Yes," Faith replied.

"And as such, you know a lot of the people who live in Freedom?"

"That's right."

"How many customers do you have during a day?"

Faith twisted her fingers together in her lap. "That's difficult to say," she said.

"Why? Why would it be? Can't you just count trans-actions? X number of cash register tickets equals X number of customers."

Faith swallowed again. "Well, yes. But it's rarely that cut and dry. We go into the register several times a day for petty cash, for change, to give a refund. You know."

"Actually no, I don't." Detective Ingram's dark brown eyes studied her. "I'm sure you know what your work-load is for a given day. Break it up into breakfast, lunch and dinner for me."

"I think we may serve seventy people between 6:00 a.m. and 10:00 a.m. on a good day. Lunch is probably a hundred or so, and then dinner could be anywhere from sixty to eighty on a weeknight to almost a hundred and fifty on a busy weekend."

"Okay. That wasn't so hard, was it?" Ingram smiled at Faith, who'd already decided she didn't like the woman.

"So, in a given week, you might see quite a few townspeople come through your café. Is that safe to say?"

"Yes," Faith answered.

"And hear a lot of what they're talking about?"

"I suppose."

"So what's your opinion of the attitude of the people of Freedom toward Governor Lockhart?"

"I think the people here are like people everywhere," Faith said, frowning at the woman. "There are those who love her, those who can't stand her and those who are pretty neutral."

Ingram nodded. "Let's talk about the ones who can't stand the governor. Who are they?"

"I'm sorry?"

"Come on, Ms. Scott. It's a simple question. Tell me the names of the people in town who dislike the governor."

"I don't understand why you're asking me all this."

"I apologize if you don't understand, but in truth, it's not necessary for you to understand why these questions are being asked. You just need to answer them."

Faith wished Matt were here. She wanted to ask him if this detective was entitled to her answers. "I'm not comfortable naming names," she said in a last-ditch effort to avoid answering.

Ingram frowned. "Ms. Scott. I came out here as a courtesy to you because you've just had a baby, but we can certainly move this interview to Amarillo."

"No! No," Faith said quickly. With a sick sense of dread pressing on her chest, she told the detective about the conversations she heard during each day.

"Okay," Detective Ingram said when she finished. "Now let's talk about Rory Stockett. When did you first meet him?"

Faith winced at Rory's name, but she'd known this was coming. This was the reason the policewoman was here.

She thought back. "About a year and a half ago now. He showed up one morning for breakfast. He said he was working on a job in the area."

"And you two started seeing each other?"

"That's right."

"And when did you become intimate?"

Faith felt her face heat up. "How is that relevant?" she snapped.

Detective Ingram lifted her chin and stared at her. "Please just answer the question."

She doubled her hands into fists and then flexed her fingers. "A couple of weeks after we first met," she said shortly.

"What were Mr. Stockett's political views? How did he feel about Governor Lockhart?"

This elicited a wry chuckle from Faith. "Rory— political views? Rory's worldview is *very* limited." She twirled a finger around her head. "It extends about this far from his nose."

"So he never talked politics? Never mentioned the governor?"

"No."

Ingram sat back and folded her arms. "That answer is not acceptable."

Faith stared at the woman. "Well, I apologize, but it's the answer. I've never known Rory Stockett to focus on anything but himself."

"So if he's not interested in politics, why do you think he shot at the governor? What makes you so certain that the man in that blurry, grainy picture is Rory Stockett?"

Faith spread her hands. "I have no clue why he'd shoot at the governor, unless—" she paused, then spread her hands "—it would have to be for money." She explained about Rory's gambling, his proposal and the fake ring, the loan and his persuasive charm.

"And why are you so sure the man in the film footage is Stockett?"

"Because of his hair. He has a patch of white hair on the left side of his head, behind his ear. It's about an inch in diameter, and it shows up plainly, even in that awful photo."

"Just one more question, Ms. Scott. You've made no secret of the fact that Rory Stockett is your baby's father and that he ran out on you after bilking you out of a sizable amount of money." The detective was getting into her setup and obviously looking forward to her big question. "Why shouldn't we assume that you're setting him up to take the fall for the shooting as revenge for what he did to you?"

Faith heard Kaleigh start to whimper and mentally thanked her baby girl for the interruption. She'd had about enough of Detective Mary Anne Ingram. She stood and looked down at her.

"I can't think of a single reason why you shouldn't assume that," she said. "All I can tell you is if you knew me, you'd know I'm not a vindictive person. My baby needs me. Are we done?"

The detective stood and adjusted her jacket. "For now. But let me stress that you don't leave town for *any* reason."

"Don't worry," Faith retorted. "I have a new baby and a café to run. I'm not going anywhere."

As Matt pulled into the parking lot of a gas station on the outskirts of town, he spotted the black Land Rover with the license plate he'd memorized. It was parked on the dark side of the station.

He was here because he'd called the number on the piece of paper Bellows had given him. He wasn't surprised that it wasn't the Department of Motor Vehicles. The voice that answered had said nothing. The conversation had been terse, to say the least.

"Bart Bellows gave me this number."

"Yeah?"

"I need to speak to the man who visited the Talk of the Town Café on Thursday."

"Yeah?"

"Can we meet at the gas station west of town at five o'clock today?"

"Eight."

Then the line had gone dead.

As he parked next to the passenger side of the Land Rover, the big bald man got out, closed the car door and leaned against it. He was dressed in another dark suit, and this time he wore dark sunglasses. Matt wondered how he'd been able to see to drive with those dark glasses on. He got out of the pickup and walked over to lean against the Land Rover next to the bigger man.

For a few moments, neither of them said a word. Finally, the man said, "Yeah?"

Matt suppressed a smile, wondering if the man had practiced his *yeahs* in front of a mirror. He had the almost uncontrollable urge to reply in single syllables, but he quelled it.

"I've got the money Ms. Scott owes you," he said, reaching into his back pocket.

"Yeah?" the man's head turned slightly toward him.

"Yeah," he answered, handing over the envelope.

The bald man fanned through the bills, and then he stuck the envelope into his inside coat pocket. "Thanks," he said, straightening up.

"Hang on a minute. Bart Bellows thought you could help us find someone."

"Bellows?" the man said, appearing to stare off into

space. He reached into his jacket pocket and pulled out a toothpick and stuck it in his mouth.

"Yeah," Matt replied. "Rory Stockett."

"Why?"

"Mr. Bellows believes Stockett has some answers about the town hall meeting."

The bald man chewed on his toothpick for a while. "Stockett's an idiot," he finally said, pushing the toothpick to the corner of his mouth.

"No argument from me," Matt responded. "But being an idiot is no excuse." He was rewarded with a twisting of the man's lips into an ugly grimace. He assumed it was supposed to be a smile.

Then the man straightened and adjusted his suit and smoothed his tie. "Stockett owes a lot of money to a dangerous man," he said as he opened the car door.

"Wait! What dangerous man?"

The other man shook his head slowly. "Can't tell you that. All I can say is if the man wanted Stockett to do something for him, Stockett wouldn't be able to refuse."

"I need more than that—" Matt started, but the bald man got into the Land Rover and closed the door.

Matt stepped away from the vehicle as its engine turned over. The big SUV pulled away, leaving him standing there.

Stockett wouldn't be able to refuse.

That could mean anything. Matt watched the vehicle's rear lights until it disappeared around a curve in the road. Then he climbed into his pickup and pulled out his phone to call Bellows and report, but just as he was about to press the number, the phone rang.

"Yeah?" he answered, then smiled wryly and shook his head. "This is Soarez," he continued.

"Matt, it's Bernie Hale. We may have a live one."

"Where?" Matt asked, glancing in the direction the Land Rover had gone.

"In Amarillo. A man was brought into Northwest Texas Hospital. He's been beaten up. No ID. The emergency room director called the police, and they called me. They say he matches Faith's description of Stockett."

"What does the man say?"

Hale grunted. "Apparently he's not talking."

"What about his hair?"

"Not sure. He's got a scalp wound that's bled all over the place. Want to take a ride with me?"

Matt looked at his watch. It was almost eight-thirty. "I'm at the gas station. I'll meet you at the hospital. Then if you need to stay, I can get back to the café."

"Sounds good."

"Sheriff? Do you think it's Stockett?"

"Beat up? Left in an alley? Refusing to answer questions? Wouldn't surprise me."

"Yeah. Me either. I'll see you there." Matt hung up, pulled out of the station and headed toward Amarillo. He dialed Faith's cell phone.

She answered on the first ring. "Matt?"

"Hey," he answered, hearing the stress in her voice, even with all the background noise in the café. "What's the matter? Everything okay?"

"No," she said, sounding more angry than upset. "They sent a detective to interrogate me this afternoon."

Matt winced. "I know, hon. I'm sorry. What did—?"

"She accused me of setting Rory up because he ran out on me."

"I don't think—"

"No, Molly. The chicken goes to table twelve. Table ten had the beef stew and cheesy biscuits."

"What are you doing working?"

"I'm feeling fine—great, as a matter of fact. All I'm doing is being hostess. I'm sitting here with Kaleigh, who's sleeping through the entire dinner rush."

"I thought you were supposed to take it easy."

"Do we have a bad connection? Because I just said I was sitting down. Will you be here soon?"

"Probably not for a couple of hours. I've got to run into Amarillo. They've picked up a man who matches your description of Stockett."

"What?" Faith said. "They arrested Rory?"

"Not sure. The man's not talking. I'm going with Sheriff Hale to question him. Let me talk to Glo."

"Glo? Why?"

He knew that Faith wouldn't like him asking Glo to babysit her, but he didn't care. He wasn't about to leave her alone. There was a good chance the man at the hospital wasn't Stockett. "Faith—"

"Okay," she snapped. "Hang on."

He drove, listening to the clanging of dishes and silverware and the drone of people talking.

"Matt? What's up?" It was Glo.

"Glo, I've got to go into Amarillo with the Sheriff. Stay with Faith until I get back, will you?"

"Sure. No problem. I'll just sack out on your couch."

"Great. I'll wake you when I get in." Matt glanced

at the dashboard clock. "I'm hoping it'll be before eleven."

"You're driving into Amarillo? Good luck with getting back here before midnight," Glo said. "But don't worry. I'll take care of the girls."

"Thanks, Glo. I owe you."

"You sure do."

Matt hung up and inched his speed up to fifteen miles above the speed limit. If they stopped him, he could claim he was working with the Amarillo police to catch the man who tried to kill Governor Lockhart. It probably wouldn't work if he said he was in a hurry to get back to a woman who had just had a baby by another man and who had more reasons than she knew of not to trust him.

Chapter Fourteen

"The kettle's on," Glo called from the kitchen. "As soon as you're finished feeding the baby and putting her to bed, we'll have some herbal tea."

Herbal tea sounded good to Faith. She looked down at her daughter, who was nursing hungrily. "When you get through, Kaleigh, Mommy's going to have some tea," she whispered. "That's right, she is."

She relaxed back in the rocking chair and closed her eyes, basking in her love for this tiny thing she'd carried inside her for so long. She was happy, content.

Until Matt's face rose in her mind. Immediately she opened her eyes, banishing the image, and looked back down at her baby. "We don't need a man, do we Kaleigh?" she cooed. "No, we don't. No, we don't."

Kaleigh's bright blue eyes opened, and she looked at Faith and made a contented little sound.

"That's right, Kaleigh. I'm glad you agree." Faith touched Kaleigh's pert little nose and whispered to her until a sound startled her.

"Glo? What was that?" she called. "Did that sound come from downstairs?"

Glo didn't answer, but at that instant the tea kettle

began to whistle its annoying tune. Faith resolved to buy a kettle that was quiet.

Kaleigh nursed for a few more minutes, until she went to sleep with her mouth still around Faith's nipple. Gently, Faith lifted her and carried her to the bassinet and laid her down. Then she turned on the baby monitor and dropped the remote receiver in her pocket, turned off the lamp and walked out into the living room, buttoning her blouse.

"Glo?" Was she in the bathroom? She glanced at the bathroom door, but it was open. "Where are you? I heard the tea kettle," she said as she stepped into the kitchen.

The sight that greeted her stunned her into silence. Rory was standing near the stove holding a gun. A *gun!* He was leaning against the kitchen counter, looking down at Glo, who was lying on the floor moaning. Her blond hair was matted with blood.

"Glo! Rory!" she cried. "Oh, my God, Rory! What are you doing? Are you crazy?" She rushed toward Glo.

"Don't move!" he shouted. His eyes were wide, the whites showing all the way around. He looked like a cornered, terrified animal. He swung his arm until the gun was pointed at her. Its barrel shook. "And don't call me crazy!"

She'd made that mistake before. Rory went ballistic if anyone ever called him crazy. She held up her hands, palms out, in a nonthreatening gesture. "I need to check on Glo. What did you do to her? I mean, is she shot?"

"Don't move!" Rory yelled. Placating him wasn't going to work. He'd moved far beyond his volatile, spurof-the-moment anger. She'd never seen him like this before.

Speaking of anger, Faith felt fury melting away her initial fear of him. "What are you going to do, Rory? Shoot me?"

Rory waved the gun, but Faith could see by the gesture that he was losing interest in the weapon.

Watching him, she knelt carefully and put the back of her hand against Glo's cheek. "Glo? Are you all right? Can you talk?"

"Damn it," Glo muttered and tried to push herself up to a sitting position. As she did, she moaned again and put a hand to her head. It came away streaked with blood.

Her eyes focused on Faith. "Bastard hit me," she slurred. "Didn't hear him." She shook her head gingerly. "Tea kettle."

"I know, Glo. Here," Faith said, pulling over a metal dinette chair. "Let me help you into the chair."

Rory started pacing back and forth across the tiny kitchen. It was only two strides for him. "Stop it, Faith. Leave her alone. She's fine. I need you to listen to *me!*" he shouted, still waving the gun around.

Faith held Glo's arm and helped her into the chair.

"Damn it!" Rory shrieked. He fired a shot into the ceiling.

Faith froze. Glo screamed.

"I told you to listen to me!" Rory pointed the gun at Faith. The barrel shook.

She was sure she could feel heat coming off the barrel. "O-okay, Rory," she said in a voice that cracked with fear. "I'm listening."

He raved as he paced. "I got to get out of town. Got

to get away tonight. They're going to kill me, Faith. *Kill* me. But it wasn't my fault. No. It wasn't my fault."

Faith winced every time the gun barrel swung her way. His forefinger was on the trigger. She didn't know much about guns but she did know from watching TV that some of them had what the characters called hair trigger, and they could go off at the least touch. Didn't Rory know that? Because to her, it looked like Rory was squeezing awfully hard on that trigger.

"Rory, you've got to calm down. If you hurt somebody with that gun, you could go to jail."

"Hah!" Rory stopped and punctuated his words with the gun's barrel. "You don't know anything. I'm going to jail anyway. They screwed me, Faith. They screwed me good. Oh, God!" He resumed his pacing.

Glo, sitting in the dinette chair, raised her head and took a long breath. "Son of a bitch," she said, touching the gash on her head tentatively. "Rory Stockett, you put that gun down right now." Glo's words were brave, but her face was a sickly gray.

Rory turned the gun on her. "You whiny old maid, you shut up or next time I won't just hit you on the head. I'll use the business end of this gun and put a bullet right through you."

"I hope they do put you in jail," Glo muttered. "Better yet, *under* the jail."

"I'm warning you, you old bag!" Rory shouted.

"Rory," Faith said evenly. "Tell me what's wrong, and I'll do whatever I can to help."

Rory's face had gone darker. Faith was terrified that he was going to snap any minute and shoot all of them. Glo's taunts weren't helping.

"Rory," she said, taking a step toward him with her

arms outstretched and her palms up. "Just tell me what I can do. I'll do anything I can to help you. You're my baby's father, after all." She hadn't wanted to say that. She'd rather just forget about him and be thankful that he wasn't the fatherly type.

Rory looked at her. "That's right," he said in a slightly calmer voice. "I am. And I'll tell you something else. No two-bit wetback's going to come in here and stake his claim on you and that baby. You're mine. Both of you. Right?"

For an instant, the gun barrel slumped downward. "Oh, Faith. I thought I'd lost you. I was so scared you were going to get hurt."

"Hurt?" Faith frowned. "Hurt how? What are you talking about?"

"I tried to warn you. I told you to stay away from the governor."

"Oh, my God, Rory! *You* threw that brick!"

"I was trying to warn you! Don't you get it?" He waved the gun again. "I was protecting you. Now you've got to help me. If they catch up to me they're going to kill me."

Faith tried to make sense of Rory's raving. "Who's going to kill you, Rory? What are you talking about?"

"I don't have time for this, Faith. Where are your car keys?"

"My car keys?" Faith repeated. "Oh, of course! You can get away in my car? I'll sign the title over to you. Then if you're stopped, it'll be legitimate."

He looked at her narrowly. "Get away. Lay low for a while. Yeah! That's what I've got to do." His eyes lost their wild animal look.

"Yeah. I know what I need. Where's your key to the basement, Faith? I need some money."

"Money? No, Rory. I don't have any. You pretty well cleaned me out."

"Don't B.S. me Faith. I know you've got cash stashed in the safe. You always do. You told me, remember?"

Of all the things Faith had told Rory in the months they were together, naturally the one he remembered was her offhand comment that she kept a couple of thousand dollars in the safe in case of emergency.

"Come on. I don't have much time. I need that money, Faith."

She shook her head, but before she could say anything else, he took a step toward her and pressed the barrel of the gun directly against the back of her neck. "Do what I say, Faith. Get a move on!"

Faith let him march her toward the door. As they left the kitchen, she looked back at Glo, sending her a silent message.

Get Kaleigh. Go down the back stairs.

Glo met her gaze, but she still looked dazed.

Please God, make her understand.

Please.

ONCE FAITH WAS FAR ENOUGH down the stairs, she saw the broken glass on the floor at the front of the diner. That explained the sound she'd heard just before the tea kettle whistled and how Rory had gotten in. He'd broken the glass on the front door and reached inside to unlock the doors.

She stepped off the last step onto the hardwood floors of the dining room. Rory nudged her forward with the barrel of the gun against her neck. "Have you got the key to the basement?" he asked.

She nodded. It was on the chain with the remote receiver for the baby monitor. She reached into her pocket and found the monitor. She needed to turn it off before Glo or the baby made a sound and reminded Rory that he'd left them unattended. Her thumb touched the toggle switch, and she flipped it.

Relief made her light-headed as she pulled the chain out of her pocket. With any luck, he wouldn't notice the key chain. She was afraid if he saw the baby monitor receiver on the chain that he'd remember he'd left Glo and Kaleigh upstairs.

Run, Glo. Get Kaleigh and run! Down the back stairs!

She stuck the key in the lock and turned it.

"Open it," Rory said. "Open the door and go straight down the stairs."

She complied. When she reached out her hand at the bottom of the stairs, Rory tensed and the gun barrel dug deeper into her neck, but once he realized she was turning on the lights, he relaxed a bit.

"Rory, you need to hurry if you want to get away. Matt will be home any minute." She immediately knew she'd said the wrong thing.

"Home?" Rory ground out, pushing the gun's barrel into her neck. "Home? Is that really how it is? You just had *my* baby and you're—?"

"Rory, I promise you. There's nothing between Matt and me." Liar. "He's just—" What? He's just what? She had no idea how to finish that sentence.

"Rory, what happened?" She tried to turn the tables.

"How did you get mixed up with people who want to hurt Governor Lockhart?"

"Don't ask me questions. Open the safe. Do it now!" Rory took a shaky breath. "You know how it is, Faith. I got in trouble with gambling. It's always the same. I can't get any freaking luck. I bet on a sure winner—a *sure* winner—and still lost."

Faith turned the knob on the safe with trembling hands. She went at it slowly and carefully, knowing Rory would think she was faking it if she screwed up the combination.

Where was Matt? She had no idea what time it was, but she knew it was late. *Please hurry,* she prayed.

"I had to pay off the debt, Faith," he wheedled. "I had to. So when they said I could pay it off by taking a potshot at the governor, it sounded easy as pie." He chuckled. "Your cherry pie, Faith."

She winced at the familiarity. One more turn and the safe door would be unlocked. She turned the knob slowly and felt the tumblers drop into place, but she didn't open the safe. She pretended to continue turning the dial and hoped Rory wasn't looking too closely.

"So you didn't intend to hit the bodyguard?" she asked softly.

"I didn't mean to hit anybody. It was supposed to be a scare. One shot fired toward the governor. The shooter gets away. End of story." He sighed. "But now, they're all pissed off because I hit that guard. Hell, anybody could have made that mistake. I don't think the gun was working right. I think the sights were off."

"So they're after you now?"

"Faith, I think they're going to kill me. That's why I've got to get out of here. I've got to hide from them."

He thrust the gun's barrel tight against her neck. "But I've got to have a disguise," he continued, his voice turning thoughtful.

"They'll be looking for me, expecting me to be by myself. I know. You'll come with me. We'll take your car and get a fake license plate. We'll travel as husband and wife."

Faith's heart slammed against her chest wall. "I can't go, Rory," she said, trying to sound regretful. "I've got the baby, remember?"

"No, no," he snapped. "You have to go. Glo can take care of the baby. You've got to help me. Yeah, we'll be husband and wife. Maybe we'll really get married." He paused. "Hey, what's taking so long with that safe? We've got to get out of here now."

Her heart was beating so hard and so fast that she could barely catch her breath. "Rory, no. You can't do this."

He was going to take her hostage and make her leave her baby behind. There was no time left. She couldn't count on Matt. If she was going to have any chance of stopping Rory, she was going to have to do it herself.

"I can't see to get the last number," she said, bending her head as if studying the numbers on the knob. "Can you see?" Casually, she put her hand on the safe's door handle.

"Damn it, Faith. Can't you do anything?" Rory stepped past her and up close enough so he could see the numbers. "What's the number supposed to be?" he asked, bending his head.

Immediately, Faith pulled the handle and swung the safe door open as hard and fast as she could.

A crack split the air. She'd managed to hit him in the head.

MATT DROVE AS FAST AS he dared. He muttered a curse as he glanced at the dashboard clock: eleven-thirty. He'd been later than he'd hoped getting away from the hospital in Amarillo.

The man the police had called Sheriff Hale about was a match for the forensic artist's sketch, but he wasn't Rory Stockett. That didn't mean he might not be the shooter, but it didn't mean he was either.

Two hours of questioning hadn't yielded any answers from him except his constant insistence that he didn't remember anything about who he was or what happened to him.

The police were sure he was lying about his amnesia. The doctors weren't sure. So they'd had to compromise. The physician in charge in the emergency room had admitted him to the psychiatric unit for evaluation, and the police had fingerprinted and photographed him to try and ID him. They'd also sent CSI out to comb the alley where he was found, for any clues to who he was and what had happened to him.

Matt checked the GPS system, noting that he was still eleven miles from the café. He picked up his phone from the console. He wanted to call Faith and tell her he was on his way. When he looked at it, he saw that he'd missed a call from her—not four minutes ago.

A slight apprehension fluttered in his chest. He pressed the redial button.

"Matt!"

It wasn't Faith. It was Glo. She sounded out of breath. "Dear God, Matt!"

"Glo, what's the matter?" Matt's hands tightened on the steering wheel, and his foot bore down on the accelerator. He could hear a baby crying in the background. *Kaleigh!*

"Glo, where's Faith?"

"It's Rory! He's got her! Had to get the baby out—"

"Where, Glo? The café? Did you call the sheriff?" Matt's heart was pounding. He gripped the wheel even tighter and floored the accelerator.

"No—" she panted "—just got Kaleigh out. He—he hit me on the head. Had to sit down. Dizzy."

"Is that Kaleigh crying? Glo? Is she all right?"

"Yeah. Hurry!"

"Glo, listen to me. Call the sheriff's office. Get them over to the café now!"

"Okay," Glo said, still breathing hard. "Dizzy." The line went dead.

It sounded like Glo had a concussion. He hoped Kaleigh was all right. And Faith—

Matt's pulse thrummed in his ears. Stockett had her.

He saw the lights of the gas station up ahead. He'd be at the café within a couple of minutes.

Dear God, don't let me be too late.

FAITH COULDN'T BELIEVE IT. Her quickly improvised plan to knock Rory out with the safe door had almost worked.

It had hit him on the side of the head, and he'd fallen backward against a stack of cases of soft drinks, tumbling them and losing his grip on his gun.

Faith saw the light glinting off steel about two feet from where he'd landed and maybe three feet from her. She slid over far enough so that it was in reach. She could hear Rory cursing and shoving boxes.

Her fingers closed around the cold metal, just about the time he managed to scramble up. He loomed over her, tilting his head to one side and holding a hand to his temple. Still, he managed to stomp on her hand with his loafered foot.

Hot, crushing pain stole her breath. She did her best to hold on to the gun, but Rory growled and stomped again.

She shrieked and lost her grip on the gun.

When he bent down to pick it up, he wavered and nearly fell over. That gave her a chance to scuttle backward, out of his reach. She scooted across the floor, hoping to duck behind the freezer.

Rory straightened. The gun was back in his hand, and he was pointing it at her. "You bitch. You hit me! You're going to pay for that."

He stopped and gave his head a shake, and then he eyed the safe. Faith watched him as she inched backward, closer and closer to the big freezer. He'd just noticed that the safe door was open.

"Hah!" he barked, and with a sideways glance at her and a grunt of pain, he stuck the gun in his belt and used both hands to rummage through the papers and file folders, looking for the cash she'd told him she always kept in there.

"Where is it, Faith?" he yelled. "Where's the cash? Tell me, and I'll let you go."

Faith cast about for something she could use as a weapon. Rory was too busy searching for the cash to pay close attention to her, and at least for the next few minutes he wasn't holding his gun.

"I keep the cash behind all those papers," she lied. In

fact it was in a plain manila envelope to the right of the stacks of records he was pulling out onto the floor.

What could I hit Rory with? she asked herself. All she could see were boxes and crates.

Crates. Wooden crates. Valerio had a crowbar down here somewhere that he used to open them. But where was it? She squinted. Then she saw it lying on top of an empty crate. She glanced back at Rory as she silently closed her hand around it and lifted.

He'd abandoned the stacks of papers and decided to check the manila envelope. He dug inside it and came out clutching a bundle of bills. He crowed in triumph and stuffed the bills into his pockets.

Faith's pulse was racing so fast that she could feel it all the way to her fingers and toes. She clutched the crowbar and crouched down, easing toward him.

With the cash stowed in his pockets, Rory pulled the gun from his belt. Faith lifted the heavy iron bar over her head with both hands.

At that instant, Rory became aware of her. He whirled. She swung the crowbar with all her might. He ducked backward, and she missed him.

The momentum of her swing sent her stumbling. She fell against the wall.

Rory's breath was sawing hard and fast, but he managed a laugh. "Okay then, Faith. I guess you're finally over me. I'd say coming at your fiancé with a crowbar defines the end of the relationship."

He raised the gun and pointed it at her.

Faith stared at him. How had she ever thought he loved her?

"Are you going to shoot me?" she asked, her voice quavering. "I'm the mother of your child. Kaleigh needs me." Tears streamed down her face, but they weren't for him. He wasn't worth tears. She was crying for her child—her Kaleigh.

"Give me a break, Faith. I'm not going to *shoot* you." He gave a short, sharp laugh. "Not unless I have to. I need you to help me get away." He stood over her with the gun pointed at her head. "Get up."

Faith didn't know what to do. She couldn't go with him. But what would he do if she refused? Would he shoot her?

Then she heard something. Rory heard it, too. He turned toward the stairs and then back to Faith.

"Get up!" he growled.

She didn't move. *Please, God. Let it be Matt.*

Rory shifted the gun to his left hand and grabbed her arm. He jerked her up, but he couldn't make her stand. She went limp.

"Get up, damn it!" he yelled, just as a shot rang out over Faith's head.

She screamed.

Rory jerked, then turned and fired at the top of the stairs. Her heart wrenched. She heard wood splinter.

"Freeze, Stockett."

It was Matt. Faith sobbed in relief.

But Rory jerked her up again, this time with his left arm, leaving his gun hand free. He dragged her around in front of him and crouched behind her. It didn't help that she'd tried to stay limp. He'd had no trouble picking her up and setting her down where he wanted her.

"I'll kill her," Rory yelled. "Let me out of here. Let me get away, and you can have her!"

"You're not going anywhere, Stockett. Put down that gun and let Faith go."

"No! I've got to get out of here. I've got to hide. They're going to kill me!"

"*I'm* going to kill you if you don't put down that gun." Matt's voice was low and even, a huge contrast to Rory's panicked shrieking.

"Faith," Matt said. "I'm going to turn on a high-powered flashlight. When I do, I want you to duck. Make yourself as small as possible and cover your head. Okay?"

"Shut up, Soarez!" Rory yelled. "Stop talking to her. I swear I'll shoot her. I swear!"

"No, you won't."

Matt's voice was so calm, so assured. Faith hoped he was right. "Okay," she said, her voice cracking.

The light flared. Faith ducked and shrank down as close to the floor as she could.

Rory screamed in rage and jumped up, shoving her out of the way. He raised his gun, but a shot rang out before he got his arm up. His scream of rage turned into a yelp of pain, and his gun hit the floor with a thud.

At that instant, Faith's world turned into chaos. People seemed to appear from every direction, pouring into her basement like floodwaters.

Matt jumped down the stairs and grabbed Rory, who was still squealing and holding his bleeding hand against his chest.

A pair of strong hands grasped her shoulders and set her upright, then handed her off to somebody else, who guided her to the stairs. Yet another hand led her up the stairs to the dining room.

Once she emerged, she saw that the hand belonged to Deputy Appleton. Had he led her up the stairs? Or had he met her at the top? She couldn't think straight. Her head kept echoing with gunshots.

She tried to thank him, but she couldn't speak. Every time she opened her mouth, she started crying.

Chapter Fifteen

As Sheriff Hale led Rory Stockett away in handcuffs, Matt pushed his way through the crowd of pajama-clad onlookers to the ambulance where Deputy Appleton had told him Faith was being examined.

He grimaced with pain every time he put his weight on his right knee. He'd come down hard on it when he'd leaped down the basement stairs. As soon as he had a chance, he needed to ice it down.

But right now he was worried about Faith. She'd already been through so much, and now she'd been taken hostage by the father of her baby, who'd held a gun to her head and threatened her life.

Matt felt the unwelcome weight of failure on his shoulders. He should have been there for her. Sheriff Hale could have gone to Amarillo alone to question the suspect.

As he limped toward the ambulance, the crowd parted, and he saw Faith sitting on the back of the vehicle with Kaleigh in her arms. The flashing red lights made her blond hair shine like spun gold. She and her baby looked like an exquisite, rose-tinted painting of a mother and child.

Inside the ambulance, Glo was lying on a stretcher

and complaining loudly to anyone who would listen that she was *not* an invalid and she did *not* need to go to the hospital. A tired-looking paramedic was trying to get an IV started in her arm.

"Hey," Matt said to Faith once he got close enough.

She glanced up at him without speaking, then looked back down at Kaleigh.

"Hey, Faith," he said again. "What did the paramedics say?"

She moved her shoulders in a tiny shrug and brushed her fingers across Kaleigh's little forehead.

Matt frowned. What was the matter with her? Was she hurt? Was Kaleigh? He glanced around and saw a second paramedic with a stethoscope slung around his neck, talking to Deputy Appleton.

Matt went over to them.

Deputy Appleton introduced him to the paramedic, whose name was Ed.

"What's wrong with Faith?" he asked without preliminaries. "Is she hurt? What about the baby?"

Ed raised his hands, palm outward. "Whoa," he said and chuckled. "Wait a minute. Faith, the young blond mother? She's doing okay. Scared, maybe a little bit in shock. I gave her a mild sedative so she can relax and sleep tonight."

"She wasn't injured? Stockett didn't hurt her?"

"She's going to have trouble with her right hand for a while. Looks like he stomped on it, but that's all." Ed wiped his face. "Baby's fine, too. Glo, the older woman, has a pretty serious concussion. We're taking her to the hospital for observation."

"So can I take Faith and the baby up to her apartment? Is she free to go?" He addressed that question both to Ed and to Deputy Appleton.

Both nodded. Appleton added, "I questioned her a little, but we can wait to do a formal interview." He looked at his watch. "Maybe tomorrow?"

Matt nodded and shook both their hands. Then he headed back over to the ambulance.

"Faith," he said, crouching down in front of her. "I'm going to take you upstairs, so you and Kaleigh can rest. Okay?"

She nodded and stood.

"Do you want me to take her?" he asked, straightening up.

"No," she said quickly, shaking her head. "I've got her."

Matt put his arm around Faith's waist once they got to the stairs. She immediately tensed. Something inside him twisted in pain. Was she afraid of him? What had gone on down there in that basement to make her wary of him touching her?

Once they got to the landing, Matt pulled out his key and unlocked the door, then stood back to let Faith enter first.

She turned at the door. "Thank you," she said tonelessly.

"Let me help you get Kaleigh to bed," he said with a little smile. He moved to step forward into the doorway.

"Please don't," she said more loudly. "Just leave me alone." She shouldered the door shut.

Matt stood there for a few seconds, stunned. He rubbed his eyes, then wiped a hand down his face. For a moment, he considered knocking and demanding to know what was wrong.

But he didn't. Faith seemed fragile, even breakable tonight. She obviously was traumatized by her ordeal. She needed to rest and mend.

He headed down the stairs, noticing that his heart hurt worse than his knee.

FOR THE NEXT TWO DAYS, Matt's waking hours were crammed with meetings, interrogations and more meetings. Bart Bellows insisted on a blow-by-blow account of the incident with Rory Stockett. Bellows and Sheriff Hale wanted Matt present every time Stockett was questioned. The Amarillo police questioned him extensively. The governor flew him down to Austin to brief her personally on everything that had happened

Matt had almost no time to himself. On Saturday afternoon, between meetings, he ran by the hospital to see Glo and found her up and getting ready to leave.

"They finally discharged me," she declared. "And about time. I've got cats to take care of and a job to go to."

"I'm glad you're okay, Glo," Matt said. "You were so brave, to get Kaleigh away from the diner like you did, and you with a concussion."

"Well," Glo's cheeks turned pink. "I love Faith and Kaleigh like they were my own," she said, her voice choking up. "I don't know what I'd do if something happened to them."

"Have you seen Faith? Since the other night, I mean?"

"She came by." Glo shook her head. "Poor thing. Blames herself for everything."

"That's nonsense," Matt retorted.

"I know that and you know that, but she's got to work it out for herself. She needs time." Glo paused for a second. "Speaking of time, when exactly are you planning to tell her—and the rest of us—just exactly who you are?"

Matt felt his face grow warm. "Who have you been talking to?" he asked her.

"Huh. The sheriff. The mayor. The *dog catcher*. Everybody knows you're working for Bart Bellows and not on any construction project either."

"Does Faith know?"

"I'd be real surprised if she didn't."

"I know I screwed up, Glo. Do you think she can ever forgive me for lying to her?"

Glo eyed him closely. "I'll be damned," she said. "You're head over heels, aren't you?" She grinned. "I knew you were attracted to her, and it's obvious how much you love that baby, but this is serious isn't it?"

Matt nodded miserably. "I want to marry her, Glo. I want to take care of her and Kaleigh. I'm not sure how I can live without them. But I'm afraid she thinks I'm worse than Stockett."

To his dismay, Glo didn't disagree with him. "Let's hope once she gets some rest and can think clearly that she can tell the difference between a silk purse and a sow's ear."

Matt left the hospital as frustrated as he'd been before he'd talked to Glo. He'd hoped she'd be able to give him some insight about Faith.

He almost went by the diner, but he was due back at the CSAI headquarters in an hour for a wrap up discussion about the latest threats to Governor Lockhart.

When he finally saw Faith, he wanted to have plenty of time to talk to her.

He needed plenty of time to convince her that she and Kaleigh should spend the rest of their lives with him.

FAITH ROCKED KAYLAIGH and hummed a lullaby. The sweet baby powder scent of her daughter at her breast wafted around her. The moon shining in the window of the nursery made pale designs on the hardwood floor. She felt as content as she ever had in her life. Leaning her head back against the back of the rocker, she continued humming.

Occasionally a thought would try to break through the melody, but Faith rejected it. She wanted nothing more than to be here in this moment, holding her baby. She was alive and well. Kaleigh was okay. Nothing else mattered.

That thought tried to intrude again, but she hummed louder and sang the few words she remembered. Soon she would have to return to her real life, where her work began before sunrise and didn't end until late at night, where not only did she have a café to run and bills to pay, she had a baby to take care of alone.

Soon she'd have to face each long, exhausting day alone. Matt's face rose in her mind—his shy smile, the way his brows drew down when he was worried about her, the feel of his lips on hers. Facing reality meant facing the rest of her life without him.

And she couldn't deal with that right now.

She looked down at Kaleigh and touched her tiny cheek. Right now, the whole world consisted of Kaleigh and her. For a little while longer, she could stave off reality by humming a lullaby.

THE FRONT OF THE CAFÉ was dark, but lights were on upstairs. Faith was still up. Matt had tried to wait until morning. Tomorrow was Monday, the one day of the week that the café was closed. It would make a lot more sense to go see her in the morning.

But he'd spent the evening packing up his few belongings and cleaning the apartment. He'd loaded everything into his pickup and then realized he had nothing to do. He could either sit around an empty apartment or drive to his mother's house in Amarillo.

Or go see Faith. So here he was, gazing up at her window and wondering whether she even wanted to see him.

He got out of the pickup and walked up to the front doors of the café. He could see Valerio in the kitchen. He rapped quietly. Valerio leaned around the kitchen door, glaring. Then his face lit up.

"Matteo! Come in!" Valero gestured to him.

He juggled his key ring until he found the key Faith had given him, unlocked the doors and stepped inside.

Valerio came out of the kitchen to greet him. "Matteo, I was just finishing up for the night. I'm glad to see you. Everything okay?"

"Yeah. It's been a hell of a week, but we've—the police—have a strong case against Stockett. He'll be in prison a long time."

"That is very good for Faith."

Matt nodded, glancing toward the stairs. "How is she?"

"She's been very quiet, spending all her time with the little baby."

"Do you think she'd mind if I go up?"

Valerio shook his head. "There is no knowing what

she or any other woman wants. Do you know that Gloriah was insulted that I did not visit her in the hospital? Even though I was the only one keeping the café open? Why would she not understand that I was busy?"

Matt grinned at Valerio. "Maybe you should ask her."

The older man untied his apron and hung it on the hook beside the kitchen door. "Maybe you should take your own advice," he said. "I am going home. Tomorrow I'm taking my boys to Amarillo. They will be up by sunrise and wanting to know when we will leave. Good night, Matteo."

"Good night, Valerio."

Matt made sure the kitchen door was locked behind Valerio, then he walked up the stairs. As he got to the top, he saw that Faith's apartment door was open. He could hear her soft, clear voice humming a lullaby.

He stepped inside, following the sweet sound, and saw that she was in the nursery. The rocking chair was facing the window, so she was sitting in profile to him, holding Kaleigh at her breast.

Love and longing overwhelmed Matt at the sight of her. Her head was bent, and she was singing to her daughter, who was greedily nursing. It was the most beautiful sight he'd ever seen.

For a long time, he just stood there, letting the serenity and beauty of the lovely mother and child wash over him. Tears pricked at his eyelids as he realized he was in the presence of the very thing he'd longed for all his life. He had no idea if Faith could ever forgive him for his lies and deceit, but if she couldn't, at least he'd been here. At least he'd had the joy of loving her for a while.

The soft, pretty melody stopped, and Faith's head turned. She'd become aware of him watching her. He froze, waiting for her reaction. God knew that he didn't want to scare her.

She glanced his way, then calmly and matter-of-factly she picked up Kaleigh and placed her on her shoulder, then covered her breast and buttoned her blouse. She patted Kaleigh on the back.

Matt tentatively moved closer, as if he were trying to rescue a frightened kitten.

"Come in, Matt," Faith said.

"Hey," he responded, walking over to her and brushing his fingers across Kaleigh's forehead, feeling her fuzzy baby hair.

For a few seconds he stood there, listening to Faith rhythmically patting Kaleigh's back. Then he pulled the armchair closer to the rocker and sat.

"How are you doing?" he asked quietly.

Faith nodded without speaking. Kaleigh burped and hiccupped.

Matt smiled for a second, then took a deep breath. "I have to apologize, Faith. I had a job to do, and part of that job was to pretend I'd drifted into town looking for work. I never meant to deceive you."

"It's okay, Matt," she said, but her voice was too calm. Almost distant.

"I want you to understand why I couldn't tell you what my real job was. I work for Bart Bellows.

"Not doing construction. He hired me as a surveillance expert and assigned me to Freedom to keep an eye out for anyone who might mean Governor Lockhart harm. I couldn't tell you—couldn't tell anyone. Sheriff Hale is the only person in town who knew who

I really was." Matt shook his head. "I didn't want to lie to you."

"I know," she said in that same calm voice.

"Faith, listen to me. This is important. I want you to know me. I want you to meet my mother and my sisters. Faith, I want you too—"

"Matt," Faith said, holding up her hand for silence. "It's okay. Really. I understand. You had a job to do and you did it. Kaleigh and I are just fine. You don't have to worry about us anymore."

Matt stood abruptly and paced. He made a conscious effort to keep his voice low and even. "Give me the baby," he said. "I want to talk to you."

"I can hold her while you talk," she said. "She's falling asleep."

"But I want to hold her, if you'll trust me."

Faith's eyebrows went up, and she met his gaze. After a couple of seconds, she nodded. "Of course I trust you."

He bent and lifted Kaleigh to his shoulder. Her sweet baby powder scent filled his heart with so much love that he felt it would burst. He tucked her into the crook of his left elbow and patted her tummy until her eyes closed and her lips parted slightly in sleep. For a moment, he couldn't tear his eyes away from her. Then he walked back over to the rocking chair and held out his hand.

Faith took it and let him pull her to her feet. She looked a little scared and she opened her mouth, but he put two fingers against her lips.

"No," he murmured. "Don't say anything. Let me get through this." He pulled her closer, until the baby was snuggled between them. "I want you and Kaleigh to marry me."

Faith's face went white. She opened her mouth again, then closed it, pressing her lips together. "Matt, I—"

"Shh. I've got really good credentials. I've got a decent job—a *permanent* job. I like babies, and I've recently learned a lot about the restaurant business." He held up three fingers, then a fourth. "And I come equipped with five babysitters."

"Five baby—?" Faith started.

"My mother and my four sisters, although Estella and Inez will be busy with college for a while. Still, they can babysit on weekends."

"I don't understand—"

He put his finger against her lips again. "Don't answer right now. I know this is sudden, and I understand that you're probably not happy with me right now, but I'm willing to wait."

He almost choked on the last word. His throat was closing up—with fear? With love? He figured it was probably both. His heart was pounding so hard he was surprised it didn't bounce right out of his chest. He held his breath, waiting for her answer.

She shook her head, and his heart sank to the floor. But then her mouth slowly stretched in a grin.

"Okay," she said, laughing. "You had me at five babysitters."

Matt stared at her, unsure if he'd heard correctly. "What? Really? You mean you will? You'll marry me?"

Faith's grin faded to a smile that carried a hint of mischief. "What woman in her right mind would turn down five babysitters? But I do have one requirement."

He couldn't wipe the smile off his own lips, even though he was a bit apprehensive about her one requirement. "What is it?" he asked. "Anything at all."

Faith's eyes sparked. "I think we should make sure we're compatible."

Matt frowned. "Compatible?"

His question was cut off as she stood on tiptoes and leaned across Kaleigh to kiss him. The baby gurgled and began to fuss.

"Why don't you put her in her crib?" she whispered in his ear.

He shivered. "Okay," he said. He took Kaleigh over to the crib and laid her in it and patted her tummy until she went back to sleep.

Faith watched him with her baby and knew that he already loved her as if she were his own. He truly was an amazing man.

When he came back over to stand in front of her, the tender expression on his face faded into a frown. "Do you think we're not compatible?"

She wrapped her arms around his neck. "Well," she drawled, nibbling on his ear, "I'd hate for us to get married and then discover that we don't fit together."

Matt's eyes went soft. "Somehow I don't think that'll happen."

"Still—" Faith smiled.

"But Faith. It's only been a week—seven days. Are you? Can you?" He stopped talking as her hands began sliding down his chest and abdomen to the button on his jeans.

"It is a little early for me, but I've been reading about—" her cheeks heated "—some of the things we *can* do."

"Th-things?"

"There are quite a few, as long as we take it nice and slow," she murmured, smiling as she unbuttoned his jeans and felt the proof of his desire for her.

"Nice and slow," Matt muttered, as his hands slipped under her blouse and caressed her full breasts. Faith moaned with pleasure as they tightened in response to his firm, yet gentle, touch.

She took his hand and led him to her bed.

"I love you so much," he whispered.

"I love you, too," she responded, her lips brushing against his as he began to caress her lightly and intimately.

"You're already turned on," he said.

Faith chuckled softly. "It must be the anticipation of those five babysitters," she murmured.

* * * * *

INTRIGUE

COMING NEXT MONTH

Available June 14, 2011

#1281 COWBOY BRIGADE
Daddy Corps
Elle James

#1282 LASSOED
Whitehorse, Montana: Chisholm Cattle Company
B.J. Daniels

#1283 BROKEN
Colby Agency: The New Equalizers
Debra Webb

#1284 THE MISSING TWIN
Guardian Angel Investigations: Lost and Found
Rita Herron

#1285 COOPER VENGEANCE
Cooper Justice: Cold Case Investigation
Paula Graves

#1286 CAPTURING THE COMMANDO
Colleen Thompson

You can find more information on upcoming
Harlequin® titles, free excerpts and more at
www.HarlequinInsideRomance.com.

HICNM0511

REQUEST YOUR FREE BOOKS!
2 FREE NOVELS PLUS 2 FREE GIFTS!

❖ Harlequin®

INTRIGUE®

BREATHTAKING ROMANTIC SUSPENSE

YES! Please send me 2 FREE Harlequin Intrigue® novels and my 2 FREE gifts (gifts are worth about $10). After receiving them, if I don't wish to receive any more books, I can return the shipping statement marked "cancel." If I don't cancel, I will receive 6 brand-new novels every month and be billed just $4.24 per book in the U.S. or $4.99 per book in Canada. That's a saving of at least 15% off the cover price! It's quite a bargain! Shipping and handling is just 50¢ per book in the U.S. and 75¢ per book in Canada.* I understand that accepting the 2 free books and gifts places me under no obligation to buy anything. I can always return a shipment and cancel at any time. Even if I never buy another book, the two free books and gifts are mine to keep forever.

182/382 HDN FC5H

Name _____ (PLEASE PRINT) _____

Address _____ Apt. # ____

City _____ State/Prov. _____ Zip/Postal Code ____

Signature (if under 18, a parent or guardian must sign)

Mail to the **Reader Service:**
IN U.S.A.: P.O. Box 1867, Buffalo, NY 14240-1867
IN CANADA: P.O. Box 609, Fort Erie, Ontario L2A 5X3
Not valid for current subscribers to Harlequin Intrigue books.

**Are you a subscriber to Harlequin Intrigue books
and want to receive the larger-print edition?
Call 1-800-873-8635 or visit www.ReaderService.com.**

* Terms and prices subject to change without notice. Prices do not include applicable taxes. Sales tax applicable in N.Y. Canadian residents will be charged applicable taxes. Offer not valid in Quebec. This offer is limited to one order per household. All orders subject to credit approval. Credit or debit balances in a customer's account(s) may be offset by any other outstanding balance owed by or to the customer. Please allow 4 to 6 weeks for delivery. Offer available while quantities last.

Your Privacy—The Reader Service is committed to protecting your privacy. Our Privacy Policy is available online at www.ReaderService.com or upon request from the Reader Service.

We make a portion of our mailing list available to reputable third parties that offer products we believe may interest you. If you prefer that we not exchange your name with third parties, or if you wish to clarify or modify your communication preferences, please visit us at www.ReaderService.com/consumerschoice or write to us at Reader Service Preference Service, P.O. Box 9062, Buffalo, NY 14269. Include your complete name and address.

HI11

Harlequin® Blaze™ brings you
New York Times *and* USA TODAY *bestselling author*
Vicki Lewis Thompson with three new steamy titles
from the bestselling miniseries SONS OF CHANCE

Chance isn't just the last name of these rugged
Wyoming cowboys—it's their motto, too!

Read on for a sneak peek at the first title,
SHOULD'VE BEEN A COWBOY

Available June 2011 only from Harlequin® Blaze™.

"THANKS FOR NOT TURNING ON THE LIGHTS," Tyler said. "I'm a mess."

"Not in my book." Even in low light, Alex had a good view of her yellow shirt plastered to her body. It was all he could do not to reach for her, mud and all. But the next move needed to be hers, not his.

She slicked her wet hair back and squeezed some water out of the ends as she glanced upward. "I like the sound of the rain on a tin roof."

"Me, too."

She met his gaze briefly and looked away. "Where's the sink?"

"At the far end, beyond the last stall."

Tyler's running shoes squished as she walked down the aisle between the rows of stalls. She glanced sideways at Alex. "So how much of a cowboy are you these days? Do you ride the range and stuff?"

"I ride." He liked being able to say that. "Why?"

"Just wondered. Last summer, you were still a city boy. You even told me you weren't the cowboy type, but you're...different now."

He wasn't sure if that was a good thing or a bad thing. Maybe she preferred city boys to cowboys. "How am I different?"

"Well, you dress differently, and your hair's a little longer. Your face seems a little more chiseled, but maybe that's because of your hair. Also, there's something else, something harder to define, an attitude..."

"Are you saying I have an attitude?"

"Not in a bad way. It's more like a quiet confidence."

He was flattered, but still he had to laugh. "I just admitted a while ago that I have all kinds of doubts about this event tomorrow. That doesn't seem like quiet confidence to me."

"This isn't about your job, it's about...your..." She took a deep breath. "It's about your sex appeal, okay? I have no business talking about it, because it will only make me want to do things I shouldn't do." She started toward the end of the barn. "Now, where's that sink? We need to get cleaned up and go back to the house. Dinner is probably ready, and I—"

He spun her around and pulled her into his arms, mud and all. "Let's do those things." Then he kissed her, knowing that she would kiss him back, knowing that this time he would take that kiss where he wanted it to go. And she would let him.

Follow Tyler and Alex's wild adventures in
SHOULD'VE BEEN A COWBOY
Available June 2011 only from Harlequin® Blaze™
wherever books are sold.